Tales of Action.

DICK WILLOUGHBY

TALES OF ACTION

By MEN OF LETTERS

Edited by L. A. G. STRONG

KNIGHTS AT BAY. *By* PHILIP LINDSAY.
DICK WILLOUGHBY. *By* C. DAY LEWIS.
FORTNIGHT SOUTH OF SKYE. *By* L. A. G. STRONG.
THE KITE. *By* REX WARNER.
FIRE IN THE ICE. *By* A. D. DIVINE.

¶ " VERY GOOD BOOKS "—*The Listener.*

CHAINED ON THE GALLEYS

DICK WILLOUGHBY

By C. DAY LEWIS

BASIL BLACKWELL · OXFORD

First printed, September 1933
Reprinted 1936
Reprinted 1946

Printed in Great Britain by
Henderson & Spalding
London, W.1

CONTENTS

v

LIST OF ILLUSTRATIONS

PART ONE
WILLOUGHBY HALL

CHAPTER I

DICK woke up with that warm, comfortable feeling you have when you know there is something nice before you and you're too sleepy to remember what it is. He unpinned and pulled back the bed-curtains: it was like coming out of a cave; his eyes dazzled with a white glare pouring in off snow, and he exclaimed joyfully, "Christmas Day!"

Snow always reminded him of Christmas, whenever it came, because it made everything look like those fine sugar confections, moulded into the shapes of houses, trees, birds and animals, which his mother only made at Christmastide. Dick wrapped the counterpane round him, and put his foot down gingerly to the rush-strown floor, like a bather getting into water. It was just as cold. But he plucked up courage, ran over to the window and snuggled up on the window-seat in his counterpane, to watch Christmas Day awaking.

The air was sleepy still with snow, and all movement on earth hushed; the cowman and his herd moving into the home-meadow seemed to be walking on cushions: a horseman galloping down the lane was galloping over a feather bed; thrushes and sparrows were sitting dumb with cold on the low box hedges of the herb garden below Dick's window. It must be like this to be deaf, he thought: till suddenly a cock in the yard set up a frantic alarum, and as if that had broken some spell the sun came out with a wink and a jovial burst of singing came round the corner of the house, followed by a giant of a man with a flaming red beard and a horse saddled and bridled.

Dick drummed on the window and called out, "Martin!"

9

"Good-morrow, Master Richard!" hailed the man, in a voice that matched his person. "What! not abroad yet, thou bed-worm, thou scobberlotcher!" and leaning down rolled a snowball in his massive hands, but desisted at the last moment from throwing it at Dick's window lest it should enter by mistake the adjoining room, where his father and mother slept; and flung it instead with great shrewdness at Sally, the pretty serving-maid, who was sweeping the snow away from the top flight of broad front steps.

"Marry, come up, thou tun of a booby," cried she in high glee; "that hairy comet of thine, that holly-bush thou grow'st to keep thy neck warm for the rope med frighten Spaniards, but not a Dorset maiden!" And she advanced upon him and shook the snow-laden besom over his head till he was enveloped in a miniature blizzard.

In the course of these operations Dick heard the curtains of his father's room pulled aside, and his father came along the passage to bid him good-morning. Sir Richard Willoughby was short and spare, birdlike in his walk, his hooked nose and his bright-glancing eyes; the friend of Drake and Hawkins, ten years ago but little less dreaded by Spanish captains than they: he had retired from sea and settled on his estate at Lyme Canonicorum in Dorset after losing his right arm in the attack of San Miguel. "Though little loss it was to me," he used to say, "for I never had need to write aught but my name; and as for a sword and a horse—I warrant I can manage them as well with the one hand as the other"—a statement which not a few high-mettled animals and vagabond bullies had since repented of calling into question.

Sir Richard came through the curtain of his son's door ready for his morning ride, in cloak, high boots and feathered hat. But there seemed something bigger than

the usual riding crop in the hand under the cloak, and something more than the usual smile of greeting on his face.

"Dick," he said, "thou art nigh fifteen: wilt be a man
soon, and 'tis time thou learnedst to wear a man's steel.
Here is thy Christmas gift." And he produced from under
the cloak a sword and belt of superb workmanship; at
the sight of them Dick forgot his new title of "man"
and behaved like the boy he still was, fastening the belt
round himself, counterpane and all, making passes at
imaginary Spaniards and trying to see himself in a six-
inch square of looking-glass propped upon the mantel-
piece, all at the same time.

"My son," his father chid him gently, "abate thy
spirits awhile. Come, sit by me. Look out of window,"
and he pointed to the terraces and gardens and the
meadows of Dorset beyond that rose and fell under their
coverlet of snow; "my father and his father looked out
upon that same prospect. This house is built on the bones
of our ancestors: some day 'twill all be thine. See that
thou deserve well of it. Thy brothers are all dead, and
thou alone art left to protect thy mother if I should die."

"Why, father——"

"Nay, my son, bear with me yet a little. Death cometh
sooner than later in these troublous times: plot and
plague are deadlier enemies than the Dons. So I would
have thee swear on this sword of thine to be faithful ever
to thy Sovereign Mistress the Queen and to be true and
gentle to all thou lovest."

Dick swore the oath with a full heart and felt he was
now really a man. And his father, who was much too
wise to break in on this new, sober mood of his son,
kissed him lightly and squeezed his arm and trod with his
light step out of the room and out of the house, where
Dick saw him talking awhile with Martin before he set

out on his ride. There were his two heroes: his father,
slight, tough as steel, swift as a rapier, a legend, almost
before his death, on the Spanish Main; and Martin, slow-
moving, ponderous, strong and trusty as an oak, his beard
jutting out like a fiery defiance to fate: he had been Sir
Richard's master gunner, and his eye was as true as his
heart.

Sir Richard now swung up on to the horse and galloped
off over the meads, the snow jetting up behind his swaying, debonair figure. Dick watched him out of sight,
pondering the words he had spoken. What was it, he
wondered, that made his father different from all other
men he had met? From the courtiers who sometimes
stayed in the tapestried guest-chambers, en route between
London and Plymouth, maybe? From good Sir Herbert
and the other local squires? From fat Master Rudgeley,
his tutor? Even from Martin? Was it that he could out-
do each of them at his own profession? Martin told many
a tale of tight corners when his own gloom had been
blown away by the serene gales of Sir Richard's courage.
Dick knew that his father could quote more of Virgil than
Rudgeley and bring down more game than Sir Herbert.
And his mother told him that at singing a song or turning a sonnet he was the match of any courtier alive, for
all his droll quips about being unable to write more than
his name.

Yet it was not just in doing things better than anyone
else that Sir Richard was different. It was not really in
doing things at all. It was something about the man
himself. Dick remembered his father telling him once
about a fine sword he had once had, perfectly welded,
perfectly balanced, perfect to the eye: and his father
saying: " 'Tis like with men as it is with swords; the
craftsman puts the best metal and all his skill into each

one; but once or twice in his life he puts the spirit of the
fire into one too, and then he has worked not a sword but
a miracle." Dick thought it must be that fiery spirit,
burning unseen within him, that made his father so
different from other men. But what could he have meant
by "plot and plague"? Of course there were plots afoot:
when were there not? The Counter-Reformation was
active, but so were Walsingham and Burghley; besides, it
was the Queen the Catholics hated, not any retired sea-
captain. As for the plague, it was common enough in all
conscience; had his brothers not died of it? But it was in
the towns that it claimed most of its victims. And any-
how, it was not like his father to worry about that sort of
thing. Yet there was no doubt that his father was changed
of late; he looked drawn sometimes; would sigh and
shake his head and bite his lip; was, for him, at times
almost irritable. Could he have had some forewarning,
some unearthly messenger of woe? Dick had heard one
serving-man tell another of the White Child that always
came to the Willoughbys as a warning of a death in the
family.

Supposing his father died. Dick looked out across the
fruitful fields and orchards; he could see the smoke of the
village over the brow of the hill and hear the rattle and
stamping of oxen in neighbouring stalls borne over the
quiet snow. All that fair land would be his; but, though
his father had said he was a man now, he felt very small
and helpless in the face of the prospect; he knew he
would give all that inheritance—nay, a hundred such—to
keep his father alive. But these were vapourish whimsies.
Of course his father wasn't going to die. He shook himself and, jumping to his feet, went to the lavender-sweet
drawers of the great oak press to take out his best festival
clothes.

CHAPTER II

FULLY dressed, he went out into the long passage. Down the great stairs, through the hall where soon the Christmas banquet was to be held, vacant now except for the motes of dust dancing in the sunlight that streamed obliquely through a window, coloured by the Willoughby arms painted upon it; and into the buttery, where he got a flagon of warm spiced ale, and broke his fast, dipping fingers of bread into it. But, thinking of the feast to come at eleven of the clock, he ate and drank sparingly, though it was yet but little after nine.

From the buttery he wandered into the kitchen. Here everything was in a scurry, like an ant-hill. The cook was watching two monstrous sides of beef turning on the spits in front of two roaring fires; Dick's mother was superintending the making of elaborate jellies and pasties; for in these days the mistress of the house was wont to take the more skilled cooking into her own hands: and scullions were darting about with pans and platters, rare saucers, condiments and herbs, sweating, jostling each other, and muttering imprecations. Dick kissed his mother, then stood about snuffing with relish the various odours, till the cook roundly told him to be off or she would hang him on one of the spits and serve up roast kid for dinner.

So Dick decided to go in search of Martin. He peeped into the spicery, and the chandlery, where they made the dip candles that would light up the evening's entertainment. Then out into the yard at the back. This was like a little township in itself, for shops in country villages were unknown, and each manor, like each ship at sea, kept its own craftsman for every need that might arise. Dick glanced in at the wheelwrights, where one of the solid, unwieldy wheels of the great family coach was undergoing repair, amid the sweet smell of newly planed wood. Here he used to come often on wet days, when lessons were over, and learn how to turn and fashion the wood from the estate. But to-day he was too excited to do more than fiddle with an adze and get in the way of old Matt the joiner, who called him in high good humour an imp of Satan. So he contented himself with pouring a handful of sawdust down Matt's neck, to that worthy's great delight: and passing the forge, where there was no display of sparks and white-hot iron soft as cheese to watch to-day, ran Martin to earth in the stables, grooming my lady's cob.

Dick marched up and down in front of him, preening himself and showing off his new sword like one of the peacocks displaying its tail on the lawns in summer.

"Is't not fine, Martin? Wilt teach me the use of it? Would that the Spaniards might march on Willoughby Hall! We should chase them into the sea, shouldn't we, Martin?"

"Why, as to that, Master Dick, methinks a Spaniard would eat thee up at one bite. But I will teach thee the sword-play an thou wilt. Though 'tis quill and parchment thou shouldst be learning to handle, perdie, and not the weapons of war," added the bluff retainer. For Dick had been a sickly child and was but lately overtaking his strength; and, moreover, his mother wished him, her only child now, to stay at home and grow up to the government of the estate, a man of peace.

However, Martin saw the eagerness in his eye, and something of his father's imperiousness too: so he took up a thin wooden stave that was handy and showed him the first positions, and told him that if he would be a swordsman his wrist must learn to be strong as iron and flexible as a sapling. In a very few minutes Dick's sword felt as if it was of lead, and Martin had somehow spirited it thrice out of his grip and sent it tinkling on the stable floor. But Martin bade him not to lose heart, for that he was quick of eye and movement, which is the stuff of which good swordsmen are made. Every day thereafter for some weeks Martin gave Dick a lesson, at some distance from the house, "lest Mistress Willoughby should hear rumour of it": and before long Dick's sword became swift and sudden as wildfire, and Martin had perforce to put forward his best skill lest he should receive an injury.

But on this first day Dick soon gave over, panting with exhaustion, and, sitting down on a heap of hay, put to Martin the question that had been nagging at his mind all the morning and for some days past.

"Martin, is all well with my father? He seems strange of late: sits mute at meat; flies out in anger; communes darkly with himself. Hast not perceived it, Martin?"

"Why, here's a coil, Dick," said Martin slowly, fingering his huge beard; "here's a coil indeed. 'Tis nothing, I tell thee. Belike he's pining for the old days on shipboard and the golden treasures of the West."

"He is not ill, then, or afeared of aught, thinkest thou?"

"Afeared!" shouted Martin with a thunderous laugh, yet as though glad to turn the conversation. "Sir Richard afeared! Why, I have seen him sail his ship under the guns of a fort, and when the Dons shot down our mainmast and it smashed through the deck at his feet, he did but call for a bowl of rose-water to wash the dust off his hands. Sir Richard afeared! Why, indeed thou pratest like an innocent." And Martin went on rumbling with deep laughter like one of his own cannonades.

Reassured by this, Dick began questioning him about gunnery, a subject of which both could never weary. While they were talking, Elias, the head verderer, came in and stood listening with a sour smile on his thin lips.

"And I tell thee, Dick," Martin was saying, "we are babes yet in our knowledge of guns and powder. We can send a ball scarce a mile from our heaviest piece. But who knows men may not learn to make ordnance that will throw it two miles or more?"

"Nay, thou'lt soon be wounding a foe out of sight altogether, like the black witches," broke in Elias scornfully, "or thou wouldst if thy shot could reach as far as thy tongue, thou great bombard!"

"How, vermin-conqueror? Thou murderer of moles and baby conies! Waggest thy shrivelled tongue at me? Couldst sink a galleon with those wooden toys of thine?" retorted Martin, pointing at the great bow and cloth-yard shafts the verderer was carrying.

"Ha! thou mayest prate of thy culverins and demi-culverins, that are fit but to batter holes in walls. Marry, 'tis all noise and no art. Show me the ordnance that could do this."

And Elias planted his legs astride and drew shaft to ear. "Mark that cushat," he said, pointing to a dove flying fast above the copse on the hillside. A twang, a hiss, something like a streak of silver lightning seemed to pass through the bird; there was a flurry of feathers, and the dove fell circling to the ploughland a hundred yards away.

"Aye, 'tis a pretty trick enough," grumbled Martin, "but——"

"But me no buts," exclaimed Elias; "thou'lt send for the bowman to win thy victories yet. The Queen herself, they say, favoureth archery, as Good King Harry did, and would pass a new law in Parliament to keep the art alive, but that she is so pestered by these fire-eating captains to spend money on match and powder and all that devil's bag of tricks."

Furious at this aspersion on his beloved admirals, Martin roared: " Why, thou parcel of cat-gut, if Drake and Grenville and their like kept not the Spaniards from these shores, thou'dst be running from them howling for thy mother, for all that feathered trumpery of thine!"

" Run, forsooth! *Thou* couldst not hope to escape that way, thou beer-logged bulk, not if King Philip and all the devils of the pit were on thy heels."

And the wily old verderer suggested that, to prove their respective paces, they should run to the fallen cushat, each place his hat beside it, and run back. Dick started them. But, after running a little way, Elias feigned to be blown and give up the race, and returned to the starting-point. Martin placed his hat beside the bird and ran back in great triumph. But while he was getting his wind, Elias took up his bow, and before Martin realized what he was about shot three arrows high into the air in as many seconds. Dick and Martin watched them open-mouthed. Up and up they went: then paused in air; then turned; then rained down on the earth: the first stuck quivering a foot from the hat; the other two transfixed brim and crown.

Martin leapt towards Elias. "My hat, my best hat, that I gave a silver angel for at Sherborne fair! Why, thou mess of skin and bone, we'll see who can drill the larger holes." And he snatched up his sword, and the dispute would have ended in the spilling of blood, had not a drumming of hooves nearby announced the return of Sir Richard from his ride.

CHAPTER III

DICK ran into the house and up to his room, to put on
his new best suit, the tight doublet of saffron colour, the
cambric ruff, the short knee breeches and long hose, and
shoes with big pom-poms on them. Then washed hands
and face in the pewter ewer, with a ball of sweet-scented
soap made after his mother's recipe, and dried himself on
the damask roller towel. Looking through the windows
he saw some guests arriving: Sir Herbert Digby and his
family; other neighbouring squires; village worthies. So
he went down into the Long Gallery, where they were
used to sit when there was company, his father and
mother following. Never, he thought, had he seen his
mother look so beautiful; her golden hair orderly in its
golden coif; moving stiff and stately in her green velvet
gown billowing out over the farthingale, the bodice tight
and stiff-pointed. She would have seemed strange indeed
to modern eyes, rather like a bell walking, but Dick
thought her fair enough to be a queen.

Nor would modern eyes altogether approve of the great
gallery which Dick thought so fine, though to an English-
man of a hundred years before it would have seemed a
miracle of comfort. The huge fire that roared up the
chimney like an autumn gale left the greater part of the
gallery cold as the weather outside, and they had to bring
the settles close in front of it. These and the few chairs
were heavy and not upholstered, a multitude of cushions
being used to make the sitting on them less uncomfortable. Dick and the younger members of the party sat
down on the cushions which were strewn about the floor.
But the gay dresses and chatter of the company, the bright

19

colours of painted woodwork and of the new tapestries
which stirred faintly in the draughts that ran along the
wall, made the scene as colourful and animated as were
the gallant folk who took part in it.

Soon they all went down into the great hall. Sir
Richard and his lady, with the most honoured guests, sat
on carved chairs at the high table; Dick and their children
on stools beside them. The rest of the company disposed
themselves at tables running down the hall at right angles.
Great salt-cellars of silver, a foot high, marked the place
at table below which the meaner guests should sit, and
there was considerable scuffling among the village
worthies as to which should be entitled to sit above the
salt. Then Master Rudgeley gabbled a long Latin grace,
his hands folded upon his capacious belly and one eye
roving the while towards the door, wherein waited servants bearing a great boar's head, tusks and all, smoking
savourly upon its huge dish.

What shouts and clapping now as the boar's head came
in triumphantly! What a din as the company fell to with
knife and spoon! How majestic the mien of the butler
pouring claret, malmsey, sack and rhenish wine into the
Venetian glasses and silver goblets at the high table! How
brave the gleam of firelight on silver, and the dull glowing pewter! There were Martin and Elias, their quarrel
forgotten quite, pledging each other in brimming beechen
bowls of cider. And as for fat Master Rudgeley—that
good clerk hacked his way through beef, mutton and
veal, through pork and pasty, through fish, flesh and fowl
as valiantly as Achilles through the serried ranks of
Trojans. Men ate then, as they lived, with an heroic
appetite. Dick, too, plied knife and finger till he could
no more; and even then found innumerable crevices that
could be filled up with marchpane and comfits.

Only when he had satisfied himself that one mouthful more would endanger the seams of the new doublet, which was already swelling ominously, did he desist and listen attentively to the conversation his elders were carrying on around him.

"Mark my words," bluff Sir Herbert was saying, "this realm shall never be at ease while the Queen of Scots draws breath."

"Nay, Sir Herbert," replied Squire Prendergast, "thou criest bogey where no fear is. A tender woman, and behind bars—she can work no ill."

"No ill! And hast thou forgotten the risings in the North, and my lord Duke of Norfolk was executed for treason for that he was in league with her?"

"But in good sooth there lies no danger now in that quarter. The Catholics of the North are broken, and in the South they are well-affected, the most of them."

"Well, an I were our good Sovereign I should not sleep o' nights till Mary Stuart was in her grave."

"Bethink you, sir," broke in Rudgeley, "to compass a prince's death, 'tis against the laws of God. Marry, thou'dst sleep little enough o' nights with a sovereign's blood on they conscience!"

"Rather a sovereign's blood than a nation's ruin," retorted Sir Herbert: "what sayest thou, my bully captain?"—turning to Sir Richard, as did all the heads at the table.

"I think thou sayest right. The Queen of Scots alive, whether she be guilty or innocent of these attempts upon our Sovereign, is a magnet for plotters; 'tis like gunpowder, that threatens to blow all to perdition when there are sparks in the air."

A young relative of Sir Richard's, a favourite of Elizabeth, here leant forward importantly, saying:

"They say at Court that my Lord Cecil doth strongly urge the Queen to sign warrant for her kinswoman's execution, but she ever evades his pleading. Surely she hath great love towards her."

"Not love, I misdoubt me," replied Sir Richard, "but policy. Mary Stuart put to death on English block would bring France about our ears, and break the line our Queen plays Philip on. The Queen must balance France and Spain against each other till England grows strong in unity."

"And the churchyard shall have us both, Richard, ere that comes to pass," exclaimed Sir Herbert. "North of Trent 'tis Percy, not Tudor, is called prince. And naught but block and stake will work loyalty among Papists."

"Rumour has it in London," said the young courtier leaning towards Sir Richard, "that thy cousin, Sir Giles Blakeney, hath a finger—and more—in the Papist conspiracies, but my Lord Walsingham can find no certain witness against him."

Had Dick been looking at his father when the name of Sir Giles, their Catholic kinsman, was mentioned, he would have seen a black cloud pass over his face. But he saw nothing: and the conversation was ended by Martin, who rose, somewhat unsteadily, in the midst of the hall, and summoned those at the lower tables to drink Sir Richard's health and his lady's. The health was drunk amid cheering and stamping and beating of tankards on tables. Sir Richard thanked them all. The quality then adjourned to the winter parlour, to make music on lute and virginals and cithern, and to sing madrigals; while the commoners fell to dancing and playing boisterous games in the hall.

Dick brought his young guests into the Long Gallery, and there they wrestled and played Prisoner's Base, Blind

Man's Buff and Barley Break. Tiring of these they started a game of Hide-and-Seek, all over the stairs and galleries and chambers, at which Dick used his superior strategic knowledge of the great rambling house to baffle all search and to leap out of dark corners on all and sundry with devastating effect. One child, Sir Herbert's youngest son, James, a lugubrious moon-faced infant of ten years, was so nerve-shattered by one of these assaults that he howled for five minutes and could only be comforted by the promise that he should be allowed to choose the next game. The lugubrious one accordingly placed thumb in mouth, and after long and deep consideration said, " Let's play at funerals."

This sombre suggestion was not exactly in accord with the mood of the party : but the promise had been given, so Dick sent two of his friends outside to gather sprigs of yew and other evergreens, while he himself with the rest routed in chests and cupboards for black drapings. When all the properties were assembled a further hitch occurred, because the lugubrious infant wanted to be both clergyman and corpse. Another explosion of grief was narrowly averted, Dick pointing out the difficulty of playing both parts and assuring him that the corpse was the most honourable and important part of the proceedings. So James was deposited in a chest and covered with black cloth and evergreens; the most stalwart of the children raised it and staggered slowly out of the front door, down the steps and into the garden, where it was proposed to conclude the ceremony by burying James in the snow.

But as they were about to lay the chest on the ground, and Michael Prendergast, as the parson, was preparing to hold a service over the body of James, a great bellow of dismay was heard proceeding from the door they had just left. This so startled the bearers that they dropped the coffin into a deep patch of snow. The corpse came to life with a frightful yell and his moon-face appeared over the side of the chest like a Jack-in-the-box; the rest of the children fled; and Dick was left to sustain the attack of a thoroughly perturbed Martin: for it was he who had caused the panic. He strode across to Dick and cuffed him soundly. Dick's eyes filled with tears, not from the pain, but from surprise; for Martin had never lost his temper with him before.

"Thou mawmet! Thou young ninney! What-a-plague dost mean by this wicked mummery?"

"Why, Martin, 'tis not wicked, surely. We did it but to please little James here. A foolish prank, maybe. Naught worse."

"Naught worse, quotha! Naught worse! Dost not know what it signifies when children play at funeral?"

"Nay, Martin, indeed I know not. What should it signify?"

But Martin, whose anger was cooled by now, would not explain its cause.

"Think no more on't, Dick. 'Tis this cursed temper of mine. Come, lad, shake hands. I did wrong to strike thee, and I'm sorry. 'Tis naught, as thou sayest."

Dick readily forgave his friend. But he was not satisfied that Martin's outburst was due to his temper. For he had read fear, as well as anger, in Martin's face. And he was determined to find out the cause of it; what evil this innocent play of theirs could forebode. But he said nothing of this to Martin; and they comforted the unhappy James and went together into the house as friends.

It being already nearly three o'clock, and the single bell of the little village church speaking in silver tone over the fields, the party set out for Divine Service; at which ceremony Master Rudgeley was sufficiently recovered from

his warfare amongst the Christmas viands to preach a
lengthy sermon on the subject of gluttony, in no way put
out of countenance by the volcanic eruptions of snoring
with which good. Sir Herbert punctuated the discourse.
When the main service was over, Dick and some of the
other children stayed behind for Catechism. Then home
again as the huge red ball of the sun fell slowly out of
sight and the air sharpened with the evening, for the
second meal of the day at five o'clock.

This banquet was a repetition of the first, save that the
number of guests had dwindled and the great hall was
alive with points of candle-flame. When it was over the
mummers came in with their blackened faces and masks
and flaunting ribbons: St. George slew the Turkish
Knight, and the Doctor and his impudent boy brought
him to life again by extracting a horse's tooth from his
mouth, and Old Bells Abub came prancing in with club
and frying pan—to the vast dismay of the moon-faced
child, whose eyes grew wide as basins at the spectacle.
When this was over, and the panting performers were
concealing their black faces behind tankards of ale, it was
the turn of the carol-singers. Harsh and jolly their voices
rose up in the familiar tunes, ending with Dick's favourite,
"Lullay, my lyking," which his mother had so often
crooned sweetly over his bed.

Then indeed it was time to say good-night. Dick went
sleepily up to his room. A wooden tub was standing there
in front of the fire, and Sally pouring cans of boiling
water therein. Dick suddenly remembered something he
must know if he was to sleep sound that night.

"Sally," he said, "tell me, what means it when children
play at funeral?"

The girl looked at him strangely, and would have
laughed the question away; but Dick stamped his foot and

put on his most domineering expression, and Sally must needs satisfy his curiosity.

"Why, Master Dick," she said, "these are but ill phantasies to trouble thy pretty head withal. But since thou must know, 'tis the country saying that 'when childer play at burial, plague and death shall befall.'"

It was a sobered Dick that climbed beneath the feather quilt and patterned counterpane that night, and his sleep was uneasy with a dream of a black-faced Master Rudgeley pursued down endless passages by a horrible figure in a mask that had "Plague" written on it in flaming letters: and now it was Dick himself that fled in dumb panic; closer, closer came the appalling pursuer: Dick screamed: the figure was on him: its claws bit into his shoulder, the other hand removed the mask, to reveal the face of—his father. And Dick awoke in agony of mind, to see his father bending over him and hear the comfort of his quiet voice. His father reassured him and brought him into his room to sleep on the truckle-bed at the foot of his own, where usually a servant slept to guard the slumbers of his master and mistress.

CHAPTER IV

SOME seven weeks after the events chronicled in the last chapter, as Dick was following Master Rudgeley through the mazes of a Latin poem, his father came in and said to the tutor:

"How fares thy pupil? Doth he deserve a holiday, think you?"

"Well enough, Sir Richard, well enough. 'Tis a good lad, thou knowest, and diligent."

"Then, Dick, thou shalt have one. To-morrow is thy birthday. I have business in London, and intend my journey thither. Wilt ride with me?"

Dick leaped up and kissed his father, flooded with wild excitement. To ride to London! The great city was as far off and fabulous to him as the Indies. And with his father! Now, verily, he was a grown man. For the rest of the day he was fidgety as a flea, and plied the tutor with a thousand questions about the city; questions which that gentleman was hard put to answer, for he had never been nearer London than Oxford.

The morrow dawned bright and windy. Dick put on his best outdoor suit and sword and the new travelling cloak his mother had made for his birthday. His father gave him a sovereign and two crowns for his purse; and there was a lovely model of a great ship beside his plate that Martin had been working upon privily for months. Dick was so excited he could scarce taste of the meat and beer for breakfast. It seemed an age before they were ready to start. But ere ten struck they were on horseback in front of the house, Dick and his father, and Martin on a stout nag bearing provision and a small trunk of necessaries for the journey. Sir Richard and Martin, beside their swords, carried dags, or small pistols; for the countryside teemed then with desperate masterless men, rogues who gave no mercy to those who could not defend themselves.

"I'll bring you back a fine gift from London," Dick cried to his mother as he set spurs to his horse. And when they came to the turn of the lane he reined in and waved to her again. He was to remember that scene all his life: the flutter of his mother's scarf on the topmost step and the brave figure of his father cantering on ahead, feather and cloak waving to the wind.

Beech boughs thrashed in the western gale, the sails of the windmill were careering merrily round, and huge galleons of cloud sailed stately across the heavens as they emerged from the lane on to the high road for London. Now the wind seemed to be blowing them towards the great city, and the tree-tops to bend and point the way. There had been rain the night before, and their horses and cloaks were soon bespattered with mud. Once Sir Richard leant over and pulled sharply at Dick's bridle, for a great hole gaped in the road in front of him, which would have endangered his neck if the horse had set foot in it: thereafter Dick paid more attention to horseman-ship and less to the many strange sights they passed on the way.

They made good progress for some hours, and took food by the roadside. But shortly after they had started again Martin's horse cast a shoe, and he had perforce to alight and lead him to the next village. This and the shoeing delayed them so much that it was dusk as they came out upon the bleak plains around Salisbury. There was no hope of reaching the town ere nightfall, so they halted at an inn whose general appearance, no less than the brush hung outside instead of a painted sign, proclaimed it to be of the meaner sort. The host, a saturnine individual with a cast in one eye, emerged and told them shortly that his best bedroom was already occupied, but the second best was at their service. Martin accompanied the ostler to the stables to see that he did not stint the horses of their corn or smear their teeth with candle-snuff to prevent them eating their fill. Dick and his father retired to their room, preceded by a servant to light the fire and pull off their boots. Mine host followed, enquiring whether they would eat at his table or take their meal in their own room. Sir Richard decided on the latter; but a quarter-hour passing and no food appearing, sent Dick down to investigate.

As Dick entered the tap-room he heard a voice saying, "We suspect——" But who was suspected, or of what, he was not destined to find out; for on his appearance the conversation stopped abruptly. There were two men only in the room, their heads close together over the remains of supper, the innkeeper and the last speaker, whose back was turned to Dick. That he was a man of rank his sombre-coloured rich clothes declared: but when he turned round Dick could see nothing but his eyes. Deep-set in a pale face, they seemed icy and remote as twin stars on a frosty night: but then they seemed to turn to needles of flame, and Dick felt as though they were burning their way into his inmost heart, laying bare every secret thereof. He could imagine those eyes following a man over the edge of the world, like cruel unerring hounds.

"Thy name, prithee, young sir?" said the stranger, in a voice as cold and keen as his eyes.

"Dick Willoughby, an it please you, sir. My father——"

"Is a brave man and an honourable," broke in the

stranger; "he hath deserved well of England." And he
looked kindly on the boy, his eye's steely glitter quite
softened, and asked him whether he was going to be a
great captain like his father when he grew up. The innkeeper went out to hurry up their dinner. The stranger
sitting down again, Dick was able to see the window ovei
his shoulder. Pressed against it on the outside, white as a
leper's, snarling malevolently at the stranger's back, was a
face. Things happened in a split second. Dick let out a
yell: the face was whisked away; and the stranger was
outside the door with a tiger's spring ere Dick drew
breath. Presently he returned, his sword drawn, his eyes
chill as daggers again.

"Gone," he replied to Dick's unspoken question.
"Wouldst know that face again? Certes, we grow accustomed to such visitors in my trade."

With which mysterious words he bade Dick good-night
and retired. Dick rejoined his father and Martin, still
trembling with the excitement of that minute. Presently
Sir Richard went downstairs, and Dick heard his voice in
conference with the stranger; but on his return he made
no reference to what had passed between them. Martin
insisted on sleeping by the door, with cold steel ready in
his hand; "for," quoth he, "mine host and his swivel eye
mislike me much. I warrant 'a is in league with all the
rogues within twenty miles and is but waiting till we shut
eye to let them in and slit our throats." However, no
blood was shed that night except Martin's, who groaned
from his pallet: "Plague on't, an Ethiopian army of fleas
is making war upon my flesh."

They arose betimes next morning, but not so early that
Dick did not see while they breakfasted a coach go lumbering out of the yard and in it the noble stranger of last
night. His quick eyes also noted a ragged-looking man

outside making a sign to some unseen individual as the coach drew away. At every turn, Dick thought, some fresh detail seemed to deepen the mystery which cloaked the stranger. But he was destined to understand some of this mystery before long.

Sir Richard's party were to horse little more than ten minutes after the coach had departed. The morning was raw, and pools of mist still hung in the hollows of the road. Dick determined to warm himself and his horse, and spurred it to a gallop, rapidly outdistancing his companions. He arrived at a turn of the road a hundred yards ahead of them; and on the lonely stretch of road, as he rounded the corner, but a score of paces in front, a grim sight met his eyes. A coach, one wheel in the ditch; one of the horses dead in the traces, the other kicking madly to be free; a man's body crumpled horribly in the road; and, his back to the side of the coach, fighting in desperate silence with sword and dagger against five ruffians—the stranger.

Dick stopped one moment aghast. Then his mind seemed to go light and clear. He shouted once to his father, drew his sword, and galloped down on the fighters like a gust of wind. At home he had often practised at the quintain—an old knightly pastime which consisted of tilting at a shield that swung on a pivot round a stout wooden post. Remembering this, he held his sword rigid in front of him, like a lance, and bent low above it, his eyes looking along the blade. Hearing the drumming of hooves, the assailants paused irresolute: but their leader, a tall, villainous-looking man, swung round to meet the charge. Dick rode straight at him; the man's weapon was swept aside by the fierce impetus of the horse; and Dick's sword pierced him through the right eye. He fell like a heavy sack; the sword, wedged in his skull, was snatched

THE RESCUE.

out of Dick's hand as he stormed past. But Dick had no further need of the weapon. The remaining scoundrels turned and fled. There were only two of them, for the stranger had leapt upon one and half hewn his head from his body, while Sir Richard had arrived in time to shoot another dead at his leader's feet.

Dick reined up and, turning his horse, dismounted. The stranger pushed over the body of Dick's victim with a disdainful foot, plucked out the sword, and returned it to Dick with a stately bow.

"Sir," he said, "I crave thy pardon for addressing thee last night as a boy. I perceive thou art a man."

Dick, feeling terribly proud—and a little sick—looked down at the corpse at his feet. The face was turned up, a wicked snarl still on the lips. It was the face he had seen at the window.

The stranger turned to Sir Richard and Martin.

"Gentlemen, I thank you. You arrived in good hour. My men fled, all but one brave fellow. And he lies there dead."

As he spoke the rest of his attendants crept up like curs, and were duly whipped by the icy tongue of their master. Two were sent back to fetch fresh horses from the inn, and Sir Richard, after assuring himself that the stranger was unhurt, prepared to ride on. But as they were moving off the latter called Dick back, and gave him a ring off his finger.

"Dick," he said, "thou hast saved a life on which our Queen deigns to set some little value. I never forget friend or enemy. Take this ring. Wear it not openly. But if ever thou shouldst have need of the Queen's secretary, do but show it at my door and thou shalt find him ready to repay the debt he owes thee."

Dick took the ring, bowed low, and galloped after his

3

father, his head in a whirl. He had killed a man: and he had won the gratitude of the great Sir Francis Walsingham. Turning the ring over in his hand, he saw the tigers, the Walsingham crest, stamped upon it. And he strove to recall all he had ever heard of that wily, fearless, remorseless man. How he had baffled every plot upon the Queen's life, lulling the craftiest of conspirators into a sense of security; then springing upon them without mercy, like one of the tigers on his coat of arms. He shivered, imagining those cat-like eyes, that could see through the darkest gloom of conspiracy, watching victims walking into the traps prepared for them. No doubt the landlord of the inn was one of his innumerable agents; for Sir Francis had no scruples how he obtained his information, and his secret service was drawn from the dregs of the populace, thieves, tricksters, wandering beggars, as well as from the best brains of the land.

No more adventures befell our travellers that day, and they lay the night at a good inn, The Pig in Armour, within forty miles of London.

CHAPTER V

Larks were trilling aloft and the jovial sun beaming down upon earth as they resumed their journey the next morning over the heathy hills of Surrey. The nearer they approached to the capital the more populous grew the highroad along which they travelled. In these days England was full of vagrants; an aimless tide of them ebbed and flowed over the face of the country, setting on the whole in the direction of London. Swarthy, earringed men, sailors whom the sea had cast up like jetsam on land; discarded soldiers, able-bodied or crippled, but reckless all; monks whose monasteries had been closed; labourers thrown out of work by the widespread substitution of sheep-farming for agriculture, or by the newly-rich merchants who bought up the farms of small-holders and felt no responsibility to the land. For every man who was willing to do honest work there were three on the roads who made a living out of knavery. Highwaymen, cut-purses, pickpockets, tricksters and beggars of every description, taking pride in their art, most of them, and scornful of those who practised some branch of roguery which they deemed baser than their own. They had their own strange jargon, unintelligible to the ears of ordinary citizens, and their own leaders, the chieftains of crime, called the "Upright Men."

The more murderous of this ruffianly army confined their activities for the most part to lonely villages and uplands. But if the traveller's life was comparatively safe in the more frequented roads, his purse was in yet greater jeopardy—as our friends were soon to discover. They were riding slowly along when they heard groans pro-

ceeding from a small copse by the wayside. Turning to
investigate they found an old man of venerable appearance rolling in agony, his clothes torn and a great red
weal over one cheek. Martin at once dismounted, and
taking a small flask of cordial from the baggage, knelt
down beside the injured man, propped his head in his
lap and applied the liquor to the contorted lips. The old
man opened his eyes, and winced grievously as he drew
himself up to a sitting posture.

"I thank you, kind sirs," he muttered faintly, "a drop
more of thine excellent cordial. A-a-ah!"

Then more vigorously:

"A murrain take the villains! Did ye fall in with them
perchance? A small rosy-faced fellow in green doublet
and a great hulking ill-featured miscreant with a black
patch over one eye? Nay, they are a league away by now,
and my purse and sapphire ring with them. May they
dance on a gibbet and roast in hell, that had no mercy to
my grey hairs! Had I my youth again they had taken
harder blows than they gave!"

And the old man staggered groaning to his feet, assisted
by Martin.

"Prithee, take my purse, good old man," quoth the
kind-hearted Martin, and fell to fumbling for it in his
clothes. But the old man stopped him at once with a
gesture of superb dignity, saying:

"'Tis passing kind in thee, and may the saints of
heaven reward thee for it. But I have no need of charity,
though thou seest me fallen into this sorry condition. Give
me my staff, and I shall make shift to convey myself to
yon village, where I have friends of substance."

And with a courtly bow and a sweet smile the old man
limped off down the road.

"A courteous old man, in sooth," said Martin, "a

bailiff perchance or a learned clerk. I trust I did him no offence in offering him money. And indeed I am well pleased he accepted not of my purse, for I have some store of crowns therein, and an amulet I bought for warding off the evil eye."

Martin reached again for his purse to show this lucky charm to Dick. But—the purse had gone.

"Hi! Hoi! Come back! Knave and coystrel! Where is my purse, thou grey-bearded runt?" yelled Martin and leapt to horse.

But the stranger gave one look round, flung away his staff and darted nimbly as a deer into the thicket, pursued by cries of "A hundred of lice go with thee! Mayest thou fry in thine own villainies!" from the baffled Martin.

Not many minutes after these stirring transactions, while Martin was yet bemoaning his loss and calling down a variety of appalling vengeances upon every limb, hair and toenail of the old man, a stranger overtook them, whose sober mien was belied by a pair of the most twinkling and quizzical eyes. To him they unfolded the recent disaster.

"Marry, ye have been well cozened," exclaimed he with a ripple of laughter. "An old man, say ye, of reverend appearance? Aye, 'tis a notable canting rogue. The constables and headboroughs of a score parishes seek to lay finger upon him. They should as soon set gyves upon a shadow or clap a will-o'-the-wisp into the pillory."

And he proceeded to expound many varieties of knavery practised upon innocent wayfarers: the shifts of Nips and Foists, the Nips who cut the purse-strings and the Foists who picked the purses with dexterous first and middle fingers and who were so contemptuous of Nips that they often would not carry a knife lest they should be taken

for one. He told them of the stratagems employed to gull
the simple public at theatres and bowling-alleys; and how
a rogue might have several accomplices, each playing his
set part in the deception.

"Then," he continued, "there be many kinds of
counterfeit cranks, such as him ye fell in with lately,
who strive to arouse pity by feigning some grievous ill.
Your palliards, to wit, that raise sores and blisters on
themselves by the applying of baneful herbs——"

"We have heard tell in our county," broke in Sir
Richard, "of Abraham-men, who counterfeit madness;
one of this sort did cozen Watt King, a farmer at Lyme
Canonicorum, and have much good provision of him
which he did sell the next day at Sherborne market with
all his wits restored. Marry, had I the handling of some
of these rogues, they had repented right soon of cheating
honest men. But what have we here?"

A strange couple came into sight as they gained the top
of a sharp incline: a stout, elderly dame, who supported
a young man of shambling gait and wild appearance.
Even as they met the pair, the young man rolled up his
eyes, shivered in every limb, and flung himself violently
down on the road, gnashing his teeth and foaming horribly at the mouth. The woman wrung her hands and
knelt at Sir Richard's stirrup, sobbing out:

"Have pity, sir, have pity! My poor son hath had these
fits ever since he was born. No leech can cure him. Oh,
well-a-day, what shall I do now, so many miles from my
home!"

Martin muttered in his beard.

"The young man hath a devil, surely," and spat and
blew his nose lest the same devil should have changed
lodgings to himself.

Sir Richard was about to hand a coin to the mother of

the epileptic, when their talkative fellow-traveller alighted from his horse, and, to the horror of our friends, proceeded to leap upon the young man and shake him viciously, as a terrier a rat. Sir Richard, whose gentle heart could ill abide to see the unfortunate maltreated, was about to intervene. But at that moment something white fell out of the man's mouth, which his assailant picked up and showed to Sir Richard.

"Soap," said he; "an old lay of these counterfeit cranks; 'twas no devil that made this rogue foam at mouth. He is no more sick than you or I;" and he kicked the fellow to his feet and drove him away, cursing, with his accomplice.

Soon after this encounter they came to a crossroads, and their companion announced that here their ways parted. But before he took leave of them, reading the unspoken thought in Sir Richard's mind, he turned to him and said:

"Sir, I perceive thou marvellest how I can know so much of knavery and be no knave myself. No, I am not one of the Upright Men, but a simple country gentleman whose fancy it is to occupy himself with the inquiring into these matters. As some delight to study astrology or alchemy, so I study roguery. An thou hast occasion to travel into Kent, thou'lt find Master Harman esteemed an honest man, I'll gage it. Thy purse is safer from me than from the Queen's Treasurer."

With which parting jest he left them. They were now within a few leagues of London, and Dick's heart beat faster to think that they would soon be within its busy gates. His racing thoughts were interrupted by a sound of trumpets on the road ahead, and he looked up to see a gorgeous cavalcade approaching. Armed horsemen and trumpeters came first. Then a gallant prancing troop of knights and ladies, their clothes and accoutrements brilliant under the cloud of dust that hung overhead. And in the midst of this troop a great coach glittering with gold and silver, drawn by milk-white steeds. Our friends moved to the side of the road and dismounted. As the coach rolled past Dick beheld a figure, stiff in fine embroidery, of a perfect majesty of carriage though sorely jolted by the springless vehicle; a glimpse of a painted face, thin lips, peevish, yet firm as a man's, and a mass of vivid auburn hair. And that was the first time Dick saw the Queen.

Behind this gay progress clattered and rumbled a line of two-wheeled carts, stretching as far as eye could reach, that carried the baggage of Elizabeth and her court upon this state visit to some nobleman's house. Dick counted over a hundred of them, and tired of counting, and still there were as many to come. It was said that the Queen's father, King Harry, used to bring a number of empty carts also in his train, in which he might bear away any such possessions of his host as took his fancy. And though Elizabeth did not indulge in this royal pillage, the expense of her sumptuous entertainment came near to ruining many an ambitious nobleman whom she deigned to visit.

Dick's head was in such a whirl with the excitement of the day and the prospects of the morrow that his first impression of London was mixed and crazy as a dream. They entered by the New Gate, and passing the prison of that name, outside which they were assailed with doleful supplication of charity for the wretches within, reached their immediate goal, that famous tavern The Three Cranes in the Vintry, hard by the river.

CHAPTER VI

Dick was awakened by cries of "Hot, fine, oatcake!" and "New brooms, green brooms!" that streamed through his window together with the early rays of the sun. It was queer, he thought, looking out, not to see over miles of country, but to have one's eye arrested by the gables of a house leaning familiarly over the street, less than a dozen feet away. And something far different from the fresh morning smell of the country assailed his nostrils when he opened the window to gaze down the street. Narrow and dark, thick with filthy refuse, it wound quickly out of sight, no traffic at present visible thereon save a mangy cur; a watchman, with bell, lantern and pointed staff, sleepily ending his rounds; and a water-bearer carrying on his shoulders a great conical tankard of water from the Thames.

When he and Martin sallied out after breakfast, Sir Richard having business elsewhere in the town, Dick remarked upon the emptiness of the streets, which he had expected to find teeming with citizens by this time.

"These are by-ways and alleys," Martin informed him, "thou'lt find folk enough in the great streets, I trow, Cheapside and the Strand. But the river is London's thoroughfare."

And so indeed Dick found it to be when they emerged presently upon the northern bank. The sullen flood sparkled with life as a road with frost. None of the coloured barges of the Court or the City Companies were on the water: but it seemed to Dick alive with smaller boats, skiffs and wherries that moved like insects over the surface, gay with the brilliant clothes of their passengers. "Eastward Ho!" bellowed a hulking great waterman in their ear: and they stepped into his wherry after some preliminary chaffering in which Martin's choleric tongue and formidable appearance played no unimportant part.

As they drew near to London Bridge, Martin, having been so enjoined by Sir Richard, bade the boatman land them at the Old Swan steps so that they might walk round to Billingsgate wharf, the arches of the bridge being so narrow that it was deemed imprudent to shoot them, even with a favourable tide and skilled watermen.

While they walked past the bridge end a skiff with three drunken madcaps in it, risking their lives for a wager, attempted the feat. Luck seemed to be with them at first, when one of the oars, not smartly enough shipped, caught the piles. The craft slewed round, was jammed by the tide against a pier, canted over, and flung its crazy crew into the water. Two scrambled out safely on to a jutting platform of wood, part of a corn-mill, but the third was whirled away down stream. Martin ran some distance below this man, plunged in, and swam to cut him off on his disastrous course. Fearfully the tawny river buffeted him. But he had learnt his business in fiercer waves than these: and presently returned towing his burden to a score of hands eagerly stretched out from the embankment.

The rescued man recovered from his sousing with remarkable rapidity, and exclaimed to the bystanders in general:

"Od's bodikins, did I not always say that liquor was man's true saviour? Had I not been full to the brim with sack already, I had swallowed enough of Father Thames to drown a regiment of mermaids."

Then, turning to Martin, added:

"My thanks to thee. I would e'en add some recompense of gold: but I am a poet and by consequence a stranger to that commodity. Howbeit, I will go straight and write a ballad in thine honour, and assure thee of immortality."

With which words he swaggered away with his sobered companions. Martin observed that a speedy mortality would be more likely his lot unless he should soon have a change of clothing, and they walked briskly back to their tavern.

On their return they found Sir Richard deep in converse with a gentleman of a stringy and parchment appearance, dressed in dark habiliments and a pair of monstrous horn spectacles which gave him the goggling look of a fish in an aquarium. The two were closeted together privately a great part of the afternoon, and it was not till supper was on the table that Dick learnt the reason for his presence—and for many things which had been troubling his mind of late.

"Dick," his father began, as they sat by the crackling fire, "thou art of age now to know certain matters that concern our fortunes. Thou hast heard me speak of Giles Blakeney, our cousin?"

"Yes, father; a Papist and a recluse I have heard him to be."

"Marry, and something worse than these, I greatly fear. He is heir, after thee, to my estates. And having small hope of coming at them by natural means, for he is of nigh three score years, he hath adopted most unnatural courses against us, his kinsmen."

"Why, surely, father—he hath made no attempt upon thy life, or mine?"

"Nay, of such I would reck little. My heart is no coward to shot and steel. But this pen-and-ink warfare, these viperish tricks o' the law—faugh, I have neither skill nor stomach for them."

" The law?"

" Aye, Sir Giles hath trumped up some fiction : claimeth that the estates rightly belong to his branch of the family : put a pack of mongrel lawyers snuffing among antique documents. In fine, he hath set a lawsuit on foot against me, and would get by quibble what is ne'er his by right."

" Then that grave gentleman who attended thee this afternoon——"

" Is my lawyer. We must needs fight the devil with his own weapons. And if Master Aitken's skill is as great as his charges, that make a sore enough leak in my purse, we should have no fear of the issue."

" Couldst thou not make petition unto the Queen? She would not see in straits one that had served her so well."

" The Queen hath but a short memory for such services. Moreover, as the wind sits now, she liketh not to take part openly against the Catholics; and my cousin is one of the most influence amongst them. Nay, we must abide the stratagems of the law and pray that victory may ensure to General Dry-as-Dust Aitken."

Sir Richard laughed and shook the cares from his brow, and soon was telling Dick some audacious enterprise of Drake on the Spanish Main, far from the cobwebs and quillets of the law.

The next day was spent in sightseeing. They visited the Tower and St. Paul's; Fleet Street, whither half the population of London seemed to have flocked, to gape at Indians, dwarfs, weird beasts, and other monstrosities conveyed by intrepid seamen from the corners of the known world; Temple Gardens, famous for their roses, two of which had begun the bloodiest civil war in England's history. In Cheapside, whose southern extent flamed like

Aladdin's Cave with the booths of goldsmiths and jewellers, Dick laid out almost his whole stock of money in a gorgeous gold ornament for his mother; and near London Wall he bought a small leather bag to be suspended on a cord beneath his clothes: in it he placed a certain ring bearing a device of tigers. Each trade confined itself to a special district, and the hubbub in these streets was terrific. Carts clattered over the cobbles, their drivers bawling to clear a way through the press; vendors shouted their wares; beggars clacked their clappers; and the animated crowd seethed and jabbered, anon breaking out in some frantic brawl of tongue or fist.

The day following, their last in London, Sir Richard took Dick for a special treat to see the bear-baiting. They crossed the river to the Paris Garden in Southwark, and entered the great wooden amphitheatre, paying a penny for admission and another penny for special places in the galleries. Perfumed courtiers in the extravagance of fashion lolled on the benches around them. The meaner seats were packed with apprentices, tradesmen, and the rag-tag of the town. A stout stake stood in the centre, and presently a bearward entered, leading a huge shambling brute, and fastened his chain to the stake. Now three mastiffs were let loose. They advanced snarling upon the bear. He gazed upon them mildly and scratched his ear. "A tame brute," thought Dick; "no fight in him, surely." But suddenly, quicker almost than eye could follow, a dog darted in and fastened his teeth in the bear's flank, another sprang at his throat, the third jumped upon him from behind. The bear, with a leisurely movement, cuffed the first dog half-way across the ring; snatched the second from his throat and broke its back; then, with a shrug of his shoulders, dislodged the third and stamped it into the sand. The crowd roared with delight, for this

SIR RICHARD AND THE BLIND BEAR.

was a famous bear, a favourite. Other mastiffs were brought on, but they could make little impression on the tough old gladiator: and soon he was led off, amidst general acclamation, for the bearward to tend his wounds.

Next a blind bear was attached, by a longer chain, to the post, and men advanced to bait him with whips. This was a sport vastly relished by the crowd. It reminded Dick of his Christmas game of Blind Man's Buff, the bear making wild swings at the air and the men ducking nimbly under his flailing claws. The brute, thoroughly infuriated, made a yet more vicious lunge. There was a rending noise. The staple was torn out of the stake, and the bear rushed wildly at the crowd, his chain clanking behind him. Now the Blind Man's Buff became a game of death. Screams and stampeding and swooning amongst the onlookers. Two men were cornered in an angle just below Dick's seat. Their only hope was to stay quite motionless. Horribly human, the bear made a tentative gesture towards them with his outstretched arms. One of the men whimpered, and the bear, striking at the sound, smashed his head like an egg. It was moving upon the other. Its slavering jaws were within a foot of his face when Sir Richard, who had jumped down into the arena, walked with his quick, bird-like step to the animal, reached up, gave his ear a hard tug; then, as the bear turned ferociously upon him, leapt away and seized the end of the chain with his one hand.

He held on to this, evading every clumsy rush and drawing the brute away towards the centre of the arena, till it suddenly seemed to lose interest and began to lick its fur. So Sir Richard delivered it over to the bearward and his assistants. The crowd, in frenzied excitement, came nearer to crushing Sir Richard to death than the bear had done. But he forced a way through them, keeping Dick close in front of him, and was outside while their plaudits were still thundering within the open circus.

As they were about to move away, a meanly dressed woman, her eyes red with weeping, plucked at Sir Richard's sleeve.

"Your honour," she exclaimed breathlessly, "my husband, Sam Cooper—he served under you in the *Good Adventure*—lieth sick unto death at home. I heard tidings you were in London and followed you hither. Oh, sir, pardon my presumption—I know not how to ask it—but if he might see you, he says, if you would but touch his hand, he would die happy."

Sir Richard never forgot an old shipmate. He sent Dick back to the tavern, and followed the woman to lend some of his lovely courage to the dying man. It was the last of many noble acts. Whether he caught it in that stricken house, or in the bear-garden—that had an ill reputation for the breeding of pestilence—he fell ill on the journey back to Dorset and died but two days after his homecoming. His wife, who nursed him with a bravery the match of his own, caught the plague from him and lingered only a short while after. And Dick was left an orphan, his whole world, that a week before had seemed happy and enduring as the walls of Willoughby Hall, tumbled in pitiful fragments at his feet.

PART TWO
CLIFFORD CASTLE

CHAPTER VII

Two months have passed since the death of Sir Richard
and his lady. Dick's heart, after the first agonies of grief,
seemed to go cold and small as a stone. Good old Sir
Herbert, who had taken the boy into his house, despaired
almost of his reason. Dick moved through the days like a
ghost, his eyes dry and unseeing, his face a mask of
tragedy; gravely accepting every kindness, but as though
refusing to come to life. Sir Herbert began to suspect that
there was something more than natural sorrow behind
Dick's icebound expression. He seemed to be brooding,
like a ghost, over some wrong done in the past and now
irrevocable. Passing Dick's room one night he heard the
boy sobbing; he opened the door quietly; Dick was
muttering to himself, between his sobs:

"Oh, why did I do it? Why did they not warn me?
God forgive me! But He will never forgive me. But it
wasn't my fault. How could I know? Yet they would
never have died if I hadn't—— Oh, my father, my mother,
I didn't mean to! And I have killed you, killed——"

And he fell a-sobbing again and beating his hands wildly
upon the wall.

"Come, Dick, my poor Dick," said the old knight,
shaking him gently by the shoulder, "there needs no talk
of killing. Thou art unmanned. Thy parents died of the
plague. Why shouldst thou call for forgiveness? Pray
rather for courage. Thy father would not have thee strike
thy colours to grief."

Still the boy wept and moaned: "It was my fault! It
was my fault!" But little by little Sir Herbert calmed him,
and like a skilful surgeon drew forth gently the cause of

51

his pain. It was the mock burial he had played on Christmas Day. Martin's anger and Sally's words about the fatal consequence omened by that innocent play had so worked upon his grief-distraught mind that at last he had come to believe himself the author of his parents' death. He was a sensitive boy, and superstition wrought fell havoc on more callous hearts than his in those demon-rid days. But the good knight soon eased him, now that his disorder was brought to light, telling him that he had been tortured by what was only an old wives' tale, and that God's wisdom was broader and brighter than they.

From that moment Dick began to live again; and though at times the black fogs of remorse rolled back upon him, for superstition is not easily to be exorcized, he fought his way manfully through them. Sir Herbert, who knew that work is the best medicine for sorrow, plied him with a hundred tasks about the house and on the estate, treating him like a man and an equal, even asking his advice on questions of policy. And Martin was always at hand, ready to talk with him about his father : for Dick was now eager to have a perfect record of him graven on his memory.

Primroses, windflowers, and daffodils were blowing in the fitful spring sunshine, and Dick's heart, like the hedgerows, putting out new life, when Sir Herbert decided that the time was ripe to talk with him about his future. Sir Giles Blakeney, his cousin, had offered to take the boy under his protection and to arrange for the government of his estate till he came of age to govern it himself. Sir Herbert would have been only too willing to keep Dick in his own house; but Sir Giles, he had to admit, had the first claim upon him. Dick was little inclined to put himself under the protection of his cousin, when he remembered the unfriendly conduct of which his father had convicted him. But Sir Herbert was evidently impressed by the letter he had received from Sir Giles, in which the writer had hinted at some legal bickering between himself and Sir Richard and said that he had determined to withdraw his suit. So a gentleman arrived in due course as overseer of Willoughby Hall, and Dick prepared to take his departure for Clifford Castle, his cousin's seat, on the western borders of Hampshire.

Great was the lamentation in Sir Herbert Digby's house that fine spring morning when Dick set out towards his new home. The good old knight, who had come to love Dick as a son, wrung his hand and pressed some golden coins into it; his buxom, bustling spouse rattled off a volley of parting injunctions about the linen which she had sewn and packed up for his use; and the moon-faced James, who had adopted Dick as his saint and hero, offered him his pet frog as a farewell present, which clammy and embarrassing gift Dick had to exercise his utmost tact in refusing.

Now he is off. The faithful Martin is to accompany him as far as Clifford Castle, and he is leading a horse that bears all Dick's movable possessions. Little he carries away from the land of his forefathers: a sword, a ring, and the gold ornament that his mother could wear but a few days were all he had to remind him of that carefree morning—how many years ago it seemed—when he waved to his mother and galloped after his father upon the London road. But, though he travelled light, his heart was as alive with memories as the rolling fields around with seed. The fiery spirit of his father seemed to ride with him, so that, as he passed the end of the lane that led to Willoughby Hall, he stiffened his lip and made a secret vow that he would never do anything of which that noble knight could be ashamed.

Their journey was uneventful, and as the evening sun declined they rode down through dark woods, and Clifford Castle came into sight a bowshot before them. Whether Dick was overtired by travelling or whether the shadow of coming events fell athwart his spirit as they trotted through the deepening shades, a feeling of gloom and revulsion fastened upon him. Sombre and silent the castle walls frowned down on the approaching travellers. Its solitary tower was outlined in black against an evening sky that raddled the moat as with the blood of tortured prisoners. A little wind moaned and died in the ancient oaks about them. Now the castle was seen to be largely in ruins, only a few lighted windows in one wing announcing that life was not quite extinct. The drawbridge was gone, and an embankment of earth had been built over the moat in front of the great postern.

As Dick and Martin approached this, the latter drew rein and beckoned his young companion close.

"Dick," he said, "I shall not see thee again privately. Thy cousin hath not need of my services, and but for thee I were little minded to seek employment in yon mass of mould and stone. I ride presently to Southampton, where I hope to take ship again and sail the seas till thou art master of thy estates. I would not leave thee, thou knowest, but so it must be. Natheless, shouldest thou have need of a friend, send word to the Rose Inn at Southampton. Ned Taylor, the landlord, is an old shipmate of thy father's and mine, and if I am on the high seas he will befriend thee. Good luck to thee, dear lad, and forget not old Martin; though he be over the horizon, his thoughts will be nigh thee."

The bluff sailor dashed a tear away and coughed with great vehemence. Then they crossed the moat and knocked upon the postern. It swung aside after some delay, reveal-

ing the figure of a man holding a massive bunch of keys.
At the sight of him Dick drew a sharp breath, and
Martin hastily crossed his fingers behind his leg. He was
tall and lean as a shadow; his arms and legs appeared of
an unnatural length contrasted with his body; his voice,
as he bade them enter, grated harshly like the key he had
turned in the lock. But it was neither limb nor voice that
caused the travellers to start back. It was the man's face.
Pitted with smallpox, deathly white as the face of a
drowned corpse it was: and the man had no nose. The
stump of it was blocked with a cork, pierced with two
quills for nostrils; and these quills made a faint eerie
whistle as he breathed.

Observing the travellers' hesitation, this apparition
broke into life.

"Hey, thou behind the beard," he addressed Martin,
"how long must I be standing here? Lead in thy horses.
My master awaits ye."

They entered the cobbled court, and Martin, after hand-
ing over the baggage to another servant, hugged Dick to
his breast and rode out again over the moat. Dick watched
him turn and wave, his red beard streaming like a flag;
then gallop away into the evening. It was the last link
with the world of his childhood snapped. A mist of tears
was before his eyes as he turned at the sound of a voice
beside him.

"Welcome, cousin Dick," it said. A girl was standing
there, hands outstretched; her face broke like a rainbow
through his tears; it was brown and delicate, and a cloud
of dark hair tumbled about it. Her red lips laughed as
she swept him a low courtesy, but her eyes observed him
keenly under the down-swept lashes. She saw a boy
whose features sorrow had moulded to an expression older
than his years. His hair was golden; and his body, though

drooping a little from weariness, had a suggestion of steely strength at the core. They looked at each other, motionless for a moment. Then she took his hand and led him into the house, saying:

"I am Sir Giles' niece Cynthia. He bids me welcome thee kindly and bring thee to him."

CHAPTER VIII

Up the broad stairs they went, lighted at meagre intervals by candles in iron sconces. Dick became aware of his heart pounding violently and a faint feeling of sickness. He was to meet his cousin, the man who had tried to filch his father's estate from him, a Papist, one darkly rumoured to be active against the Queen. What he expected to see goodness only knows; something with horns and tail and a reeking dagger in hand, I dare say. What he did see was most unalarming. As they entered the long gallery a figure arose from a joint stool by the fire and moved to meet them. A small, insignificant figure of a man, clad a little shabbily, with a sparse, greyish beard, and a nose hooked like Sir Richard's, but more pronounced. His voice had a slight lisp in it, and as he turned to lead Dick to a settle the boy noticed that he was malformed, a hunchback.

"Welcome, Dick," he said, putting his hands on the boy's shoulders that were almost on a level with his own, "my house and all therein is thine: though indeed I fear me thou wilt find it but mean quarters after Willoughby Hall."

The mention of Willoughby Hall spoilt the generosity of this speech for Dick: for he could not help recalling Sir Giles' recent designs upon it; and he answered his cousin rather stiffly. Sir Giles evidently sensed the coldness in his voice. His eyes, that had a trick of looking downward and sideward as he spoke, shot a sharp glance at the boy. He patted his sleeve and said:

"I know well there is something betwixt thee and me. I blame thee not at all. We will talk of it later. In the meantime, thou art hungered after thy journey."

He rang a small hand-bell at his elbow, and the ill-featured servitor who had met them at the gate appeared bearing a tray of food. Dick fell to with a will, and when he had finished, Cynthia waited upon him prettily with a bowl of water for him to wash his hands. Then, at a sign from Sir Giles, she withdrew. Sir Giles leant his pointed chin on the heavy ebony stick he used to assist his movements, and with downcast eyes addressed Dick :

" It were well, since we are to be of each other's company for several years, that no cause of discord should lie between us. Thou hast heard ill-report of me?"

" Nay, Sir Giles. That is—er——" stuttered Dick, taken aback by this frontal assault.

" Thou needst not dissemble, Dick. We Catholics are easy targets for calumny. Doubtless my reputation has not gone unscathed. But, I tell thee, they are vile traducers who——"

" Sir," interrupted Dick with a flare of indignation, " I am only a boy; but I hear no man miscall my father. Was it a vile calumny that thou didst essay to rob him of his estate? Did my father lie when he——?"

Sir Giles held up his hand. Dick noticed that the knuckles of the other were white on the handle of his stick. But his voice was still unruffled as he said :

" Thou mistakest me. I spoke not of Sir Richard. But since these matters are in question, I will open my heart to thee without reserve. It is true that I set on foot a lawsuit against him. I did honestly believe then that my claim was just, and my lawyers encouraged me thereto. 'Twas an unkind act, I own. I seek not to extenuate it. But, bethink thee, Dick, in what a grievous plight we Catholics stand. Every man's hand seems against us, and canst thou wonder that, when the quarry is at bay, he biteth blindly at all around? Enough of that. I have withdrawn my suit.

I am sorry it was ever undertaken. Thou must appre-
hend that I would not have received thee in my house had
I any ill-will against thee. Let us be friends. Thy hand,
cousin Dick."

Mollified by these words, and rather ashamed of his
outburst, Dick took Sir Giles' hand. It was hot and dry,
like the claw of a bird.

The fire was hot. Drowsy after the journey and the
mulled claret he had taken, Dick fell into a doze. Was he
waking or sleeping? His cousin's face was before him, yet
somehow changed. The eyes, fixed unwinking upon him;
the beaked nose; the thin lips set cruelly. He was back in
Fleet Street, staring at a vulture in a cage. The door
opened, and Dick's eyes with it. Cynthia had come in to
play backgammon. Sir Giles was smiling amiably at him
from the other side of the fire.

"Cynthia," said he, in his gentle lisp, "thou wilt be
kind to Dick? He is an orphan, now, as thou art. I am
glad thou art to have a playmate. An old man is but ill
company for young blood. But indeed I count myself for-
tunate having such as thou to lighten these gloomy walls.
And now that Dick is here my fortune is doubled."

Sir Giles stroked the girl's dark hair. It may have been
an illusion of the flickering firelight, or that Dick's facul-
ties were sharpened by the strangeness of his new surroundings; but he fancied that he detected the faintest
shudder, an almost imperceptible recoil, in the girl's slight
figure as her uncle's hand touched her. There was no
suggestion of uneasiness, however, in the lips that smiled
demurely at him over the backgammon board, or in her
merry laughter when he was twice defeated at the game.
Dick was inclined to be rueful over his defeat, for he
fancied his skill and liked to be mocked by a girl even less
than to be beaten by her. His disconsolate face tickled her

mirth but the more, and the roof rang with her madcap
laughter, which was so infectious that Dick found himself
bubbling with merriment too, his soreness quite forgotten.

So they bade Sir Giles good-night, and Cynthia lighted
Dick to his room down what seemed to him in his sleepy
state a Chinese puzzle of passages. The wind had got up
since his arrival. It rattled at the ill-fitting panes and
rustled the arras till it sounded like footsteps of one moving stealthily to some dark deed. As he snuffed the candle
and crept into the feather bed that had been warmed with
a great brass warming-pan, he heard it whiffling and hul-
labalooing round the house. Now it gave a huge, boisterous bellow, like Martin's: now it was Cynthia's laughter,
wild and thrilling: now it rose to a scream, an eldritch
weird scream, like—Dick thought as he fell asleep—the
scream of a vulture rending its prey.

He awoke, too, with the sound of wind in his ears, but
faint now and far off. It was no natural wind, though.
He opened his eyes to see the cork-nosed retainer at his
bedside, breathing sibilantly.

"Eight of the clock, Master Richard," rasped this being
in his rusty voice; "time for slugabeds to rise."

And he began to move about the room, rekindling the
fire and laying out a suit of clothes for Dick. There was
something vaguely disquieting about his movements, like
those of a wraith, a monstrous figure of nightmare. Dick
felt he might shoot up suddenly till his head touched the
roof, or the sky; or dwindle horribly so that he could
crawl like a beetle under the door. His face, too. It should
have been funny: and it was not. It was repulsive as the
face of a demon of the pit, pig-snouted, that Dick had
once seen painted in an antique book by some monk long
dead. He could not take his eyes off it. The man, aware
of the scrutiny, paused in his work and said:

"Marry, come up! Hast had thy fill of staring?"

"I mean no discourtesy," replied Dick, "but indeed I would fain know—that is to say——" he broke off, embarrassed by the man's unfriendly gaze.

"Thou wouldst fain know how I came by this snout of mine, sayest thou? Aye, 'twas ever thus. 'Tis not enough that I should be condemned to wear this remembrance of a traitor's sword all my life; but every chit of a child must e'en stare me out of countenance, or mock my affliction when I go abroad. Perchance thou wilt find a worse terror in Clifford Castle than this marred visage. Ask thy little playmate to tell thee of the Shining Leper."

The man gave Dick a most unpleasant leer, and withdrew. At breakfast that morning Dick ventured to ask his kinsman the history of this strange servant. He was told that his name was Stephen Sant, and he had been a retainer of Sir Giles for twenty years. His injury had been received while defending his master from the violence of one he had always deemed his friend; this person had attacked Sir Giles treacherously one night in London as they were returning from a carousal, and Stephen, interposing himself, had had his nose shorn away by the sword. An ingenious surgeon had saved Stephen's life and rigged him up with the monstrous appendage which so fascinated Dick.

"This injury hath soured his disposition somewhat," continued Sir Giles, "but thou must bear with his humours. He hath a faithful heart. He hath not been uncivil to thee?" he added.

Dick replied that the man's speech had indeed been something ungracious. Sir Giles may have spoken to Stephen about this, for his manner to Dick altered thereafter. Dick was not sure he did not prefer the old disagreeable gruffness; Stephen Sant now began to fawn upon him

in a sickly manner. It was rather like a toad trying to be
polite. However, Dick had few dealings with the man.
His cousin's library was open for him to browse in. A
neighbouring curate came to give him lessons; a Protestant,
rather to Dick's surprise, for he had expected some en-
deavour on Sir Giles' part to win him to the Catholic faith.
And Cynthia roamed with him all over the countryside
and the castle. He was inclined at first to be shy with her
and contemptuous of her girlish powers. But something
happened within a week of his arrival at the castle that
altered his opinions: it was to alter the course of his life
as well.

CHAPTER IX

DICK, for some reason he could not exactly state, had forborne to enquire further into a certain sinister hint Stephen Sant had let fall his first morning in the castle. Something had been said which Dick preferred to keep buried deep in his mind, out of the innocent light of day. But one afternoon, when he was talking with Cynthia, the subject of ghosts cropped up, and Dick mentioned the White Child that was said to haunt the family of Willoughby.

"Why, Dick," the girl replied, "the Blakeneys have a phantom that will match thy White Child. Hast not heard of the Shining Leper?"

"Aye, Stephen said something of it; he told me—to ask thee. Hast thou seen it? What is the history of this haunting? Art not afraid to be housed with a spectre?"

Dick tumbled out a flood of questions. Now the subject was brought to light he felt strangely unconcerned. The sun glowed mildly through the windows, brightening all within. There seemed no dark corners, no room for horror here.

Cynthia settled herself more comfortably among the cushions and took up her tale, Dick listening with rapt gaze.

"Two hundred years ago Sir Roger Blakeney, ancestor of my uncle, lived here, the proudest baron in the whole shire. But his pride was fated to a fall. He became a leper. His family shut him up in a room in the tower. His food was left outside the door every day. No one saw him after that, till a certain evening—— But I outrun my tale. He used to have a little bell, and when he wished to exercise himself about the house he would go ringing it, and all fled before the sound, for they feared to be so much as in the same room with that stricken man. Well, one evening they were all sitting in here when that door opened——"

She pointed dramatically, and Dick, looking with some misgiving over his shoulder, saw that what he had believed to be an oaken panel was indeed a door, cunningly let into the wall.

"There was no bell this time to warn them. The door opened, and the leper moved slowly into the room. Terror thrilled through the company, for the hands and the face of the leper shone; they glowed with baleful light. Hands and face, do I say? They were not hands, but stumps; no face it was, but a flat desert of flesh. The creature stalked towards his eldest son, who had been most instrumental in confining him to the tower room. The young man could not move. His father touched him, and he was stricken where he stood, a gibbering maniac the rest of his years. Then the leper turned and went out again through that door up into the tower. It was three hours before they could summon courage to follow. In the end his other sons and a neighbouring baron ascended the stairs. They saw the food untasted which had been left outside his door that morning. They broke in, and found Sir Roger dead. He had been dead a day and a night. They recognized him by his ring, for his face was eaten all away."

"And that is the door?" whispered Dick, glancing fearfully at the ill-omened panel, half expecting the Shining Leper to step through it.

"Aye. 'Twas kept locked from that hour. And the room is walled up. But I chanced to find in a secret drawer a key which fits the door. It is the only way up to the tower, and at times a mood takes me to walk upon the battlement."

"Thou wouldst not dare to go past the leper's chamber; thou, a girl? Nay, I'll believe it not."

Cynthia's dark eyes sparkled and her brow set in an ominous frown.

"I, a girl," she mimicked; "marry and I do dare. I go not to visit the spectre; on a clear day I can descry from the tower-top the sea over which my father sailed to his death."

Seeing Dick still incredulous, she ran off to her room, returning presently with a key, which she inserted into a hole in the embossed panel.

"Now," she exclaimed, turning to Dick, "though a timid girl, it seems, may not adventure yonder, 'tis doubtless a trivial feat for the far-famed valour of your majesty."

And she threw open the door with a mocking curtsy. Dick hardly dared set foot on that frightful stair; still less, though, did he dare to refuse Cynthia's challenge. He set his lip and advanced into the gloom. The staircase twirled giddily up and up. A bat flicked past his ear. His fear was not relieved by the voice of his cousin just behind him, announcing gaily that the leper was reputed still to descend these steps, heralding a death in the household. Presently they came to a small stone landing. The wall in front was faced with brick. A darker shadow seemed to envelop them here; the close, musty air seemed to grow suddenly more loathsome in Dick's nostrils. He shivered; Cynthia saw it, and in a fit of madcap bravado knocked at the brick and cried:

"Art thou awake, Sir Leper? Here is a young gentleman to see thee."

Dick's last shreds of courage fluttered away. He took to his heels and fled up the stairs, never stopping till he had flung open a wooden door and emerged on to the flat top of the tower. Then, to his final horror, he became

5

aware that something was following him. Above the racket of his pounding heart he heard footsteps, measured and muffled, ascending the staircase. He hurled himself wildly at the door. A weight began pushing against him from the other side. A voice, in cavernous tones, said:

" Sir Greatheart Willoughby, thy last hour is come. Open!"—and burst into a silver merriment of laughter. It was Cynthia.

Dick's shame and chagrin were immeasurable. He almost wished it had been the Shining Leper on the other side of the door and not Cynthia; for she proceeded mercilessly to tease and torment him, enquiring with sweet politeness whether it was wise of him to stay out in the fresh air when he was so heated with running; and whether it was the perfection of courage to leave a timid girl to the clutches of a spectre. Dick blushed hotly; bent his head in confusion. Then the girl's cruel mood changed bewilderingly to tenderness; she put her arm round Dick's shoulders, sitting down beside him on the parapet, and her gentle tongue soon healed the wounds it had made. Noticing the cord round Dick's neck, she wheedled him to tell her, as a great secret, of Sir Francis Walsingham's ring and how he had won it. He spoke reluctantly of his own part in the affray: but Cynthia was quick to imagine that it had been greater than he claimed, and her eyes shone upon him with a new light.

" Ah, would I were a man!" she cried, rising up and stretching her arms towards the distant sea that merged mysteriously with the sky beyond the last lap of land. " Then would I sail forth into the golden west and find my fortune there. Or I would go to Court and have converse with the great ones and hold the helm of State. But I am a girl, and here must I stay, mewed up like a falcon that hath a desire unto the skies."

She looked so beautiful, her gipsy-dark face thrilled with her thoughts and whipped to a rose-crimson by the wind, that Dick was fain to muster up some courtly speech and tell her that, wherever she was, adventure must be near. She tossed her head, half pleased, half impatient. Suddenly, from the woods far below, the sound of a horn came floating up to the tower. They looked over. A stag, tiny as a Noah's Ark toy, ran out of the trees, miniature hounds and horsemen close behind him. Cynthia clapped her hands.

"Oh, brave sight!" she exclaimed. "I would give my gold bracelet to be there. Thou shalt ride with me when next the hunt meets at Millhurst. Loo! Loo! After him!" she yelled to the hounds that moved so slowly and woodenly below them, her cries snatched out of her mouth and whirled away like thin leaves by the streaming wind. When the hunt had passed, Dick thought to entertain Cynthia by telling her of the bear-baiting he had seen in London. He felt somehow that it would help to re-establish himself in her esteem—his association with that scene of fashion and violence. He described it vividly : was so absorbed in living it again that he did not notice the girl's face. She broke in on him before he had reached the incident of his father's gallant rescue.

"Faugh! Have done, Dick! I care not for thy slaughter-house stories."

She was quite pale. Her nostrils curved contemptuously. Dick stammered in amazement.

"But—but, Cynthia : 'tis an ancient, honourable sport. The Queen goeth to watch it often, and her Court."

"Sport, sayest thou? Is it sport for a poor blind brute to be chained up and whipped? Butchery were a better name."

"Marry, thou pratest like a silly girl," retorted Dick,

stung by her words, "or like one of those mumping
Puritans who would forbid all games and jollity."

"I had rather be a Puritan than a torturer of helpless
brutes. They are all cowards that go to gape at such
spectacles. Cowards! Cowards!" she repeated, stamping
her foot.

Dick spoke, very slowly, his lips compressed.

"My father, then, was a coward, for that he would
watch the baiting?"

"Aye, all are cravens that watch others torment a brute
they would fly from themselves. Cravens and bullies!"
she cried wildly, a little frightened by the menace in
Dick's face.

Dick forgot that she was a girl, forgot everything but
the slight upon his dead father's honour. He sprang at her
and bore her to the ground. She wriggled and clawed,
wiry as a wild cat; but she was no match for him. He
clutched her throat and bumped her head twice, hard, on
the leaden floor. The tension of his rage suddenly
snapped. He got up, mumbling shamefaced apology.
Cynthia rose too, swift as a bent steel rod released.

"Now I know thou art a craven. So to use thy beastly
force upon a girl! I despise and hate thee. And I will
prove thee trebly a coward."

Before Dick could move, she mounted the parapet of
the tower and began to walk along it, her head high,
superb in its flush of pride. The parapet was two feet
broad; a drop of a hundred feet if nerve failed and footing
slipped. She seemed to be walking on the edge of the
world, poised on the lip of disaster.

"Come down, Cynthia, come down! I am sorry for
what I did. Oh, please come down!"

But she would not come down till she had walked right
round the four sides of the tower. Then she stepped off

the parapet, breathing easily, not speaking her challenge.
Dick knew what he must do—and knew that his nerve
would probably break. He mounted the coping; took a
few steps, careful to look straight ahead. But the strange
craving to look down overmastered him. He gave one
glance. A gulf of air yawned horribly below him; the
castle wall swept smooth and merciless, sheer down, leading his eye to the sullen surface of the moat that seemed
to be waiting for his body. Everything down there looked
so unnaturally small: like nightmare properties. They
were pulling at him. They were rushing up at him with
nightmare speed. His stomach turned right over inside
him. And just then a stronger gust of wind came at the
tower. Dick swayed. Cynthia leapt like a tigress, snatched
his sleeve, and pulled him down into safety. Then he
heard a thump beside him. She had fainted.

Dick was at his wits' end. What was he to do? He had
heard that one should burn feathers under a person's nose
when he was in a swoon. But how did one come by burnt
feathers on the bare top of a tower? And was it a swoon?
Had he done her some grievous injury in the struggle? He
took her head in his lap and called her name distractedly.
Her eyelids quivered, opened. Her eyes widened in horror;
then, seeing him safe, grew calm and happy.

"Oh, Cynthia," he cried, "have I hurt thee? Why
didst thou swoon? Art thou ill?"

The colour flooded back into her face. She rose unsteadily and looked at him in a way he could not fathom.
Then, with a queer faltering laugh, she said:

"Why did I swoon? Thou art brave, my Dick; but
thou art blind—a blind boy."

The strange creature flung her arms round his neck,
kissed him, and fled from him down the dizzy stairs.

CHAPTER X

FROM that day on Cynthia and Dick became firm friends. They both admired courage more than all the virtues, so they found plenty to admire in each other. And the shadow of death that had fallen on the tower-top remained as an invisible bond between them. They had their tiffs and bickerings: Dick was proud of spirit, Cynthia wild and wayward: but these were soon over and only made them know each other the better. Sir Giles, though his religion and physical deformity combined to make him shy of society, encouraged them to go abroad and visit the neighbours. To Dick he was uniformly kind and courteous, providing for him horses and hawks, letting him roam at will over the countryside, so that Dick soon began to know the intricate woods and the fringes of moorland beyond as well as his native Dorset.

Only one place was forbidden him—Sir Giles' own private study. He had once unwittingly entered it and seen his cousin bending over a great chest which appeared to be full of papers. Sir Giles had spun round with an oath and glared at him like a beast disturbed in its lair. But his anger seemed to subside as quickly as it had arisen, and he merely told Dick in a mild voice that he desired him never to enter this room without invitation; so Dick soon forgot the incident. The rest of the house was virgin country, asking to be explored. Many were the rainy days he and Cynthia spent adventuring through its passages and chambers: the attics, full of the mouldering treasures of the past: furniture, instruments of music, rich fabrics—relics of bygone gaiety; and the dungeons, where grimmer memorials lay and rusted: the rack, the thumbscrews, the iron rods, strange fanged monstrosities—instruments that

70

had made a whole countryside curse and blaspheme against one baron in years long ago.

Only one thing marred the pleasure of these explorings. The sinister figure of Stephen Sant was too apt to fall across their path. They would come upon his dead eyes round corners: unsounding footsteps would follow them down corridors: a darker shadow would detach itself from the darkness of some alcove—Stephen Sant. He never hindered their goings: only spoke a few words, his harsh voice grotesquely tuned to servility, and passed on —as though on some errand. Dick could scarcely complain of such behaviour: there was nothing but instinct to suggest that the servitor was not about his lawful occasions. Yet he felt he was under a kind of ghostly surveillance. Sant was like some spider watching him moving about the mazy web of the castle, biding his time.

Dick noticed that this surveillance became more intense when there were visitors at Clifford, especially if he happened to be in the passage at the end of which Sir Giles' study lay. It seemed silly; but it was as though Stephen did sentry-go there on such occasions. Visitors, indeed, were unexpectedly numerous. For a man who went out so little, Sir Giles seemed to entertain a great deal. If it could be called entertaining: for the guests never took meals with the family and departed as unobtrusively as they came. One in particular, a man with grave eyes and white hands and forehead, who wore an inexplicable air of authority, always appeared to arrive after nightfall; and he was never there the next morning. When Dick did meet him, it was only by accidental rencontre in some passage. And how he got in was a mystery, for no jangling of the postern bell ever heralded his presence in the castle.

Once, when Sir Giles was in particularly good humour, Dick ventured to approach the subject of these strange

comings and goings. His cousin was no whit perturbed
by the question, and told Dick quite frankly that his visitors were Catholics, who had—rightly or wrongly—in-
curred the enmity of the government and whom he
assisted as best he could to get out of the country. The
grave-eyed man, he added, to a further question, was a
priest—who was compelled to minister secretly to his scattered flock. The readiness and unconcern with which Sir
Giles answered set Dick's doubts at rest: he could understand now how the rumours started that whispered his
cousin to be privy to Catholic conspiracy. Apart from this,
Stephen Sant's eccentric conduct, and the number of men
employed about the castle, which seemed to Dick rather
large considering its dilapidation and the smallness of
the estate, there was nothing to give ground for suspicion.
And there was Sir Giles' constant kindness to be weighed
in the other side of the balance. Dick began to think he
must be a cruelly maligned man.

Several months after his arrival, Dick was sitting at
breakfast alone: Cynthia was visiting some friends, and
would not be back till evening. It was a Sunday, but unlike the Sundays he remembered in Dorset; for Sir Giles
paid the Queen money in default of attendance at church,
and Dick found the church sufficiently distant to warrant
his visiting it but seldom. While he ate his egg and
cracked the empty shell, as his nurse had showed him, so
that no witch might use it to convey herself across the
ocean, he pondered what he would do with his morning.
He decided to take horse and explore a remote part of the
woodland, to the east of the castle.

He rode for a couple of hours amongst the shifting
shadows of the woods and the leaves that were now turning tawny with autumn. The trees brooded peacefully
over the long turf rides: there was no life or noise, save

when a fox stole across in front of him or the wings of a frightened wood-pigeon exploded noisily amongst the branches overhead. He was about to turn his horse homeward, when he saw the roof of a hovel, the beginnings of a tiny hamlet, in a clearing to his left. Thinking to ask a drink of milk there, he rode towards it. As he came to the brink of the trees, he heard an angry jangle of voices from the other side of the cottage; so he dismounted, tied up his horse, and moved cautiously round to investigate.

A group of clownish youths, village hobbledehoys, were standing excitedly on the rank grass patch before the cottage door. They seemed to be urging each other to enter, but none was willing to take the first step. Approaching, Dick heard their conversation.

" Aye, marry, a witch she is. But last midsummer she cast her eye on my father's cow, and in a week the beast had rot i' the foot and died."

" They say she turneth herself into a chicken and doth fly up and peck parson's chin for that he allowed her not to the sacrament."

" My uncle says that once she was burnt with irons to make her confess her commerce with the Evil One. But she had swallowed the king bee of a hive, a charm against the pain, and would say naught."

" Zounds, king bee or no king bee, she'll speak if I lay hands on her!" shouted a hulking red-haired youth, their leader, and stepped aggressively towards the door.

" Have a care, Simon, have a care! Or she'll turn us all into frogs, or summon a legion of fiends upon us," muttered another.

Just then an old woman came to the door. And a gruesome enough sight she was for superstitious eyes. Ragged and unkempt, a tuft of beard on her chin, which wagged incessantly with the palsy; wandering eyes, and fingers gross and gnarled as pollard willows. Two of the gang fled outright at the sight of her. But three, bolder spirits, held their ground. Even these, daunted by the hag's uncouth appearance, dared go no further and contented themselves with curses muttered under their breath and fingers crossed. All might have been well had not a black cat jumped out of the gloom on to the old woman's shoulder. This seemed to infuriate the red-haired youth out of his cowardice.

"Ha, thou beldam trot! Thy familiar hath come to succour thee, but it shall avail thee naught. Fire cannot burn thee, mayhap. We'll see if water will not drown thee, hag-witch, thou shrivelled spawn of Satan!"

And he struck the woman a cruel blow on the face, and twisting her arm behind her back began to propel her towards an adjacent pond. Dick had watched the preliminaries with mild interest and some trepidation lest the witch should exercise her powers. But the youth's savage blow reversed his sympathies: like his father, he could not abide to see the weak oppressed. Something snapped in his brain. He sprang towards the group, swung the red-haired youth round by the shoulder and flung him to the ground. The youth yelled with fear, believing that the witch had set a goblin upon him. But, looking up and seeing only a slight lad, smaller than himself by nearly a head, he scrambled to his feet and charged at him, his upper lip rising to a snarl. One vicious blow sizzled past Dick's head; a second jarred him as though he had been struck by a stone from a sling. He landed once, with a pulpy thud, on his opponent's nose, only to be half lifted off his feet by a flailing fist that caught him behind the ear. The whole earth swung in a semicircle before his dazed senses. He had just wit enough to realize that he was no match for his enemy at fisticuffs, and gathering all his failing strength to one purpose sprang at his throat.

The bully was tumbled backwards by the fury of this assault. Dick pressed his head into the heaving chest and gripped the youth's thick neck with fingers remorseless as the jaws of a man-trap. He was fastened there, like a bull-terrier, impervious to the desperate pummelling, biting and scratching of his adversary, when the other two lads decided it was safe to take a hand in the game. One of them raised his staff and smashed it down on Dick's head. Dick felt very sick; a wave of blackness surged over him; his fingers relaxed and he crumpled beside the body he had so nearly mastered. The youth rose and kicked him twice in blind revenge. Then, believing him to be dead, they all took to their heels.

Dick's eyes opened to a darkness heavy as the darkness of his swoon. He raised his head. Pain stabbed through and through it. He groaned. A hand, with gross, gnarled fingers, set a draught of some bitter liquid to his lips. A voice quavered above him.

"Poor young gentleman, brave young gentleman, be not afeared of old Betsy. She meaneth no harm to man or beast. She is but a poor, afflicted old woman, and no worker of witchcraft."

He was in the witch's hovel. His eyes, smarting with the smoke that hung about the room, for there was no chimney—only a hole in the roof above the hearth—slowly began to take in his surroundings. The old woman was bent over a cauldron that bubbled upon the crackling sticks. He was lying on a blanket and a litter of ferns. The hag bathed his head with liquid from the cauldron, and bound it with a filthy piece of rag torn from her skirts. The herb-cordial had set the sap flowing in him again: he rose up, refreshed. He was vaguely surprised

to find that he felt no terror or disgust of the eerie old
creature. She put goat's milk and a cake of bread before
him, then poured out a little flour left from her baking
on to the rude table, and began sifting it strangely in
patterns.

"Old Betsy hath small means to recompense her deliverer," she mumbled; "natheless, though she be no
black witch, she hath power to forecast the future. What
is thy name, pretty boy?"

"Dick; Dick Willoughby."

"Thou art to be honoured and happy, Dick. I see great
ships and the smoke of battle. Gold head shall wed dark
head. But stay, there is an enemy here; a poisoned heart.
Thou must beware of stone, of wood and of water. But
thou shalt vanquish all, brave Master Dick, thou shalt
vanquish all if thou escapest one."

Her voice rose in a cackling laugh. Dick thought her
wits must be wandering, and, feeling now better able to
undertake the ride back, went outside into the wood. The
old woman followed him and helped him up on his horse.

"Young master," she said, as he was about to ride off,
"I had a son once; he would have been like thee, gallant
and kind of heart, his mother's protector. Wilt thou kiss
me once?"

Dick bent down without hesitation and kissed her. He
saw she was crying. Then he waved and rode off. He
was always wont to act thus, on impulse, without casting
about in his mind whether he ought to do such and such
a thing, whether people would approve, what would be
the result. It was some minutes after he had passed out
of hearing of the crone's repeated blessings that he recalled the legend he had read in some story book of the
young man who kissed a hideous old harridan and she
turned into a shining goddess before his eyes. He smiled

ruefully, thinking how there had been no such magic transformation of the woman he had just left. A claw of pain tore at his aching head. He slowed the horse to a walk : that jolting jog-trot was too much for him. There were miles yet to go, a stern fight against exhaustion before him. He set his teeth.

That ride was the second nightmare of his life. Pain ebbed and flowed through his bruised body : the advancing shades of evening kept pace with him. Twice he fainted, and recovered to find himself slumped forward over the mane of the horse whose instinct was carrying him home. Sometimes a fit of delirium would seize him, and the tree-trunks assumed grotesque and menacing shapes, pressing in upon the ride ahead as though they would crush horse and rider to death. After what seemed several lifetimes he came out into the open, beside one of the ruined wings of the castle. He felt so deadly sick that he dismounted to rally his forces for the last effort. He sat down against a wall, the remains of a long-abandoned cottage, on the hither side of the moat. There was a click, a whir, and he found himself tumbling down a steep underground slope, dark as Egypt's plague.

He was past all surprise; simply got to his feet and tottered along, feeling his way by the walls. These presently grew damp, and his feet squashed upon some creature of the depths. He was under the moat. Now the passage rose sharply : became steps : a door. He pushed it open and went through, moving automatic as a sleepwalker. He was in his uncle's room. He gazed about it incuriously; there was no one there. He knew where he wanted to go, the goal that had drawn him on, like a beckoning light, all that terrible evening. He staggered into Cynthia's room, stood swaying, gave her the last flicker of a smile, and pitched forward at her feet.

CHAPTER XI

For a week after this Dick lay in high fever. The wound on his head, which the fall into the secret passage had caused to bleed afresh, and the exposure to the cold evening air were nearly the end of him. But he was tough, his wiry frame full of fight. Cynthia had tended him with healing balms and clean bandages the moment he arrived: Sir Giles had carried him to bed and sent for a physician. So the day came when Dick, recovered to full consciousness, sat up on his pillows and began to forget the past week's phantasmagoria of pain and delirium. His hand went idly to his neck. He cried weakly:

"The ring! My ring! Where is it gone?"

"Do not distress thyself, dear Dick," said Cynthia from where she sat by the fire. "I have it safe. I took it from thy neck the night"—her voice faltered—"the night thou camest home."

He struggled hard with his weakness. There was something very important, something he must be reassured of. He focussed it in his tired mind.

"The ring, Cynthia: did I babble of it in delirium? Does anyone know the secret? Sir Giles? Or——"

"Aye, thou didst cry for it, finding it gone. My uncle asked me what was this ring thou didst set such value on: and knowing thou wishedst it a secret I told him 'twas a ring of thy mother's. My mind misgives me for the lie."

Dick leant back upon the pillows, calm and happy. His mind felt quite clear now, and much stronger. It moved actively to new thoughts. He began to see things with curious clearness, as through the air of a rare autumn day.

Cynthia's presence of mind in taking the ring and keeping its secret : it was more than presence of mind; it was a fine courage, a godlike quality, that must have enabled her to remember so small a thing in so great an emergency, confronted unexpectedly by himself bleeding and half dead. He couldn't imagine anyone else but his father doing a thing like that. Then he remembered that ride home : how home had meant Cynthia; how the thought of her had been like a lighted window or a landmark, helping him home, infusing supernatural endurance into his worn-out body. And looking at her, the dark eyes that dreamed in the firelight, the lovely proud carriage of her head, he realized suddenly—yet without any surprise— that he loved her and always would. The knowledge filled him with a spacious peace. There was no need to talk about it : he was very young, his future all uncharted. But he loved her, and everything would be all right, everything would be all right.

During his convalescence the boy was quite won over by his uncle's tender and continual attention. Sir Giles sat with him by the hour, telling him old Italian tales and discoursing on the mysteries of alchemy. As he spoke of the agelong search for the formula which should transmute baser metals into gold, his eyes glowed like Vulcan's fire. He found the highway to Dick's heart by asking him a hundred questions about his father, and lamenting the fact that he had never made his better acquaintance. Dick was moved by something wistful in his cousin's eyes; read an appeal for affection between the lines, so that, when next he wrote to his old friend Sir Herbert Digby, he mentioned most favourably his cousin's kindness. Strangely enough, just as he had finished the letter, Sir Giles came in and, learning to whom Dick was writing, said jokingly :

"Thou hadst better tell the worthy knight that thou

findest me not such a monster after all as fame would have me!"

Dick assured him that he had done so, and Sir Giles laid his hand lightly on the boy's golden head. What was it that made him stir restively under the hand, barely controlling an involuntary recoil? He could not say. It was something in him deeper than reason, but he dismissed it as foolish fancy, and was ashamed of such a sign of ingratitude. Only later, talking with Cynthia, he remembered the incident of his first night at the castle, when he fancied he detected a similar shrinking on the part of the girl.

"Cynthia," he said, "thou lovest thy uncle?"

"What a strange question," she replied. "Love my uncle? Surely I do." Then, more slowly, "Yes, I—I must love him indeed; his kindness—— But why dost thou ask?"

"Thou likest not his touch; is it not so?"

The girl looked at him strangely.

"Thou hast kestrel's eyes, Dick, to note so small a thing. Aye, 'tis true. Base ingratitude it seems to shrink from a protector. Yet—somehow—I cannot help it. Perchance 'tis his deformity. Nay, I know not."

"He hath never entreated thee ill?"

"Nay, he hath been ever the pattern of courtesy. But once have I seen him angered. Soon after I first came here I was walking upon the demesne, and I chanced to wander near that ruined cottage on the east side of the castle, hard by the moat. He appeared suddenly out of it, and when he saw me—— Oh, Dick, it was terrible—his face seemed to break up with anger; it was like—like a bird of prey. Yet an instant after it was placid and smiling. I thought my eyes had misled me. Verily, it was some chancy trick of the twilight."

Dick told her of the secret passage, and they decided that it must be the way by which the priest entered the castle. This would account for Sir Giles' discomposure. An alarming thought burst in on Dick's mind.

"Cynthia. Thy uncle would be enraged indeed if he found out I had discovered the passage. And surely he must know; for how else could I have got into the castle that night? My horse came not with me. Was it not found without the walls? Yet Sir Giles hath not questioned me as to my entry. 'Tis passing strange."

"Not strange, Dick. The luck ran thy way that night. The postern chanced to be open, and no one in the courtyard. They presume thou didst enter unnoticed, leave thy horse there, and pass up into my room by the ordinary way."

Dick breathed a sigh of relief. Fortune had certainly sided with him; and she seemed set fair for the future, as days and weeks passed by and no untoward event broke the pleasant monotony of his country life. But when she smiles disarmingly, she is too often preparing calamity. And so it was with Dick. Three blows were struck at him in rapid succession, each more deadly. A carefree boy was turned into a mortal hunted apparently by the blind malice of fate.

A roaring December gale was coursing through the wood and galloping madly against the crazy old castle walls. It drummed in Dick's ears as he awoke that morning and watched the huddled clouds flying in panic across heaven. It was a nice change, though, from the wan, foggy weather they had had lately, when vapours of decay arising from the moat every morning had contrasted unbearably in his mind with that sweet fragrance of wallflowers that used to greet him when he opened his window at Willoughby Hall. He dressed and went out to lean his body against the solid hedge of the wind. It was

6

early. There seemed to be no one about. Even Stephen
Sant was not plying his shadowy business in the passages.

Dick stood outside, on the inward bank of the moat,
whose livid surface looked up at him with a kind of dead
malevolence. It reminded him of the face of Stephen
Sant—the same unhealthy, impenetrable expression. He
thought, shuddering, how fearful it would be to fall into
that wicked water. He moved fascinated to the very brink.
Then the thought of how near he himself had once come
to falling in made him draw back—and saved his life.
Something was coming at him out of the sky: he knew it
an instant before the actual sound of the falling body filled
his ears. A great block of masonry crashed into the
ground at his feet, then slid with horrid deliberation into
the moat. Drops of rank water were flung up into his
face, and bubbles appeared to mark the place where his
body, too, should have been.

Dick found himself trembling all over, a cold feeling
at the pit of his stomach. He turned. His uncle's white
face looked through a ground-floor window: he was
beckoning frantically. Dick went indoors, and his uncle
pressed him to his bosom.

"Dick—I saw it all. Surely a guardian saint hath saved
thee. I had never forgiven myself if thou hadst come to
mortal harm under my protection. A curse on those who
have so persecuted me and impaired my estate that it doth
crumble about our ears. Promise me, dear lad, thou wilt
never stand beneath these walls in a high gale till I find
means to repair them: for repaired they shall be, and
that presently. 'Twere better to drain my coffers than
lose thy young life."

Dick endeavoured to lighten Sir Giles' concern, assuring him he was none the worse for the accident and
promising not to expose himself to any risk in the future.

Cynthia now came in. The crash of falling stone had not reached her ears through the massy castle walls : but Dick, excited and talkative after his escape, painted the whole incident for her in vividest colours, so that she paled and bit her trembling lip.

" Oh, Dick," she said faintly, " run no more into danger. Or, if thou must, I would—I would fain be at thy side."

The last words were spoken in such a tiny whisper that Dick was not sure he had heard aright. But the very possibility that she had uttered them made his heart leap like a greyhound unleashed. As it happens, they were to be fulfilled. She was to stand at his side in the hour of his deadliest peril.

But before this came upon him another accident befell, a thing so natural perhaps that, if it had not recalled to him certain words spoken in the witch's cottage, he might have put to it no significance whatever. He was riding by the verge of the woodlands one crisp morning early in the next year. A groom behind him, his favourite hawk on his wrist—a falcon whose sleepy-looking eyes were covered at present by the hood. The bird had leather straps attached to its legs by rings of silver—varvels, they were called—on which Dick's name was inscribed. Presently they struck out on higher ground, a spacious arena of sky above them, and beheld a heron high up, a quarter of a mile distant, beating its lonely flight home to the heronry.

In strong excitement, Dick unhooded his falcon and released the jesses. The bird blinked once solemnly, put its head on one side, then leapt superbly into the sky. At the same time the groom had released a second hawk, its mate; and together the two birds weaved their way in huge upward spirals towards the quarry. The heron, that was coming down wind at a great pace far above the tree-

tops, soon noticed his attackers and flapped his wings
more strongly to gain altitude. Up and up the three birds
soared, till now, cloud-high almost and mere dots to the
eye, the falcons had the upper berth. One óf them closed
his wings and stooped, bullet-like. The bodies merged;
came apart. The hawk had missed, and went plunging
on, braking hard with stretched wings; then struggled up
into ascendancy again.

Meanwhile the second hawk, Dick's, had taken up
position and dropped. This time hawk and heron did not
come apart. The other bird, too, stooped at the quarry;
and the three of them, a blurr of flurried wings, came
twisting and tumbling down into the heart of the woodland. Dick and the groom rode hard towards the spot
where they must have fallen. They secured their prize,
the kingly heron, the finest Dick had ever taken, and
jessed the falcons again. Then they sat down at the foot
of an oak to partake of some pasties and a bottle of wine
which the groom had brought at his saddle-bow.

While they were eating, there came a crackle from the
undergrowth in front, and a deer stepped cautiously
through the dappled shadows. Seeing them, he stood
stock-still a moment snuffing the air, and Dick bent down
to get a better view of the beast between the interposed
branches. At the same instant the deer started forward
and was gone, and something buzzed viciously over Dick's
head, its wind lifting his hair, and smacked into the tree-
trunk above him. It was the quarrel from a crossbow, a
stout, murderous, iron-shod missile. It would have split
Dick's skull as easily as a hammer would burst a nut.
The groom sprang up with an oath and plunged into the
brushwood after the sound of receding footsteps, but soon
returned from vain pursuit.

"Zounds," he panted, "the Rascal Jack may well run!

'Tis worth his neck to loose a shaft in these woods at deer or vermin. But these poaching fellows swarm in our coverts as thick as bugs in a blanket: and they reck nothing of the life of man or beast."

Dick felt too shaken to resume their sport, so they set off back to the castle. A phrase was dancing like a rout of devils in his brain: "Thou must beware of stone, of wood, and of water!" Stone and wood. Had the witch really said it, or had it been a fiction of his belaboured head? How strangely the words had foreshadowed the truth. Well, he was past two of the hazards now. Water remained; a menace crouching dimly in the dark places of the future. Peering into it, he felt a vague disquietude. And then: "Thou shalt vanquish all, if thou escapest one." One what? One danger? If so, he was safe, for he had escaped twain. Might it not, though, be one—his flesh crawled with fear—one person? The witch had spoken of a "poisoned heart." Had he some unknown enemy? Some enemy who invisibly directed disaster against him? But who? The livid face of Stephen Sant rose up before him. Could it be he? There was no other living man he could suspect.

The answer to this riddle was open for him to read, had his eyes not still been dazed by the shadow of death, when he returned to the castle. Sir Giles was at the postern; his face went white and drawn as with a spasm of fear when he saw the boy.

"Why, Dick, thou art early back. Is aught amiss?"

Dick told his cousin of his escape, and Sir Giles vowed he would set all the constables of the shire hotfoot after the careless archer. But he was never apprehended, and Dick was to curse his own blindness before long in that he had not seen the solution of the riddle, the answer that had been written for a few moments as large as life.

CHAPTER XII

IT was two months after Dick's sixteenth birthday. For day after day, it seemed, the rain had been falling, a dismal curtain between him and the outdoor sports which spring had promised. But yester-evening the heavens had relented; a great rainbow had come to bridge the watery earth; and to-day Dick and Cynthia were to ride forth to the hunt that was meeting some miles away at Millhurst. Just as they were about to set off, a brave sight in their bright, billowy hunting clothes, Sir Giles handed Dick a sealed letter.

"I pray thee, on thy return from the assembly, leave this letter at the house of Master Inglesby at Whinstead. 'Tis but a mile out of thy straight road back, and it concerns matters of importance. Fare ye well! May ye find a lusty great stag and hear the mort ere sundown."

Sir Giles lisped a gentle farewell, and turned back into the house. Dick was indeed to hear the mort ere sundown : but over no lusty stag. It was a bad day for scent, and the hounds—never in the best of condition at this period—were sluggish after their long inactivity. Twice a stag was harboured, and the curling horn of the huntsman sang through the wet woods; twice the noble company spurred to a gallop; and twice the hounds, after a brief run, lost the scent. It was a disappointing day. By three of the afternoon the hunt was dispersed, and Cynthia and Dick were riding homeward. They left Sir Giles' letter at Master Inglesby's, and struck into the rough track that led back to Clifford.

"Cheerily, Dick, cheerily!" cried Cynthia. "Why, thou art melancholy as a gib-cat. Hast swallowed a love potion? Or is my company so distasteful to thee?"

Dick tried to respond to her gaiety, but his laughter ran false and there was a wry twist to his smile. He was feeling more in sympathy with hunted beasts than with jolly hunters. So must the stag feel, he thought, when the horn's threat is carried to his ears, the homely woods are turned all hostile, and the whole world seems to be riding him down. Dick's nerve had been strained, more seriously than he knew, by the two blows which fortune had aimed so implacably against him. And there was the third yet in store, the apprehension of it sapping away at his courage.

A distant roar increased in their ears. They were approaching a place of ill-omen, the bones of a hamlet whose inhabitants had been wiped out two hundred years before by the Black Death. No one had dared to settle down again on that unlucky site. Nettles grew where cottages had crumbled away, and the mill-race turned no industrious wheel. A wooden bridge crossed the river a hundred yards above the mill-race that foamed and roared now with the weight of recent floods. Cynthia, bored by Dick's mumpish mood, began to canter ahead. A strange cloud of uneasiness loomed up in the boy's heart: he spurred to overtake her. As he was drawing abreast of her the bridge appeared in front. And Dick knew suddenly, with absolute conviction, that there he was face to face at last with his third and culminating hazard. But Cynthia, hearing the hooves drumming at her elbow, imagined that he intended a race: so she, too, put spurs to her horse. Dick called wildly; his voice was drowned by the thunder of the galloping. An instinct, a sixth sense, told him beyond reach of doubt that death waited at the bridge.

So began that extraordinary race: the one riding in innocent rivalry, the other with disaster numbing his heart. Slowly Dick's horse crept past. He yelled warnings to Cynthia; her excitement stopped her ears. He tried to pluck at her bridle, but she madly struck down his hand with her whip. Now he was in front. He might have reined up his horse in the girl's way: there was just room. But madness seized him too. Some resistless power drove him at the bridge, as though he were determined to prove the presence of the doom that lurked there. He felt a curious relief, like a schoolboy's relief when the cupboard of canes is opened and he is going to get it over quickly, as he hurtled on to the narrow bridge a dozen yards ahead of Cynthia.

A rending crack. The horse's head canted up mountainously, its forefeet scrabbling at the wooden planks, its hindquarters loose over a void where the bridge had been. Very, very slowly, it seemed to Dick, he slipped off its back, and fell—a little apart from the horse—into the yellow, hurrying river. A cry rang remotely. Was it his own voice? The waters rose up and stifled him: they echoed like a horn in his ears. It was the mort. He came to the surface again and wondered—rather petulantly— why he had never learnt swimming. Then, as the roar of the mill-race rose louder, he struggled and floundered frantically, and went under a second and a third time. His lungs fought against the invading water: the sides of his head were being pressed agonizingly outwards: it was going to burst. Then the storm of pain suddenly stopped, and during the lull a single flash of vision shot through his brain. He was back outside the postern the afternoon of the accident in the wood. There stood Sir Giles: his face grew pale with a spasm of fear as he saw Dick returning. With deliberate logic Dick's drowning mind read the answer to his riddle. Sir Giles could not have known of the crossbow bolt that had missed him: yet fear had been written on his face. Sir Giles could not have known of the accident—unless he had planned it.

Dick rose for the third time. His hand struck something solid, gripped frenziedly. A small, strong hand fastened on his collar. A cool voice spoke courage in his ear.

Cynthia had seen the bridge give way, and reined in with magnificent horsemanship, her mare rising up on hind legs and pawing at the sky as she felt the iron curb check her. Then Cynthia had turned, galloped nearly half-way down to the weir, and spurred the shrinking brute into the river. The mare, after her first hesitation, implicitly trusting her mistress, swam bravely up against the merciless current, just holding her own against it; and between them they intercepted Dick's body as it was swirled downstream. But the struggle was not yet over. The mare was tiring, and Dick's weight heavy upon her flank. She began to drift towards the mill-race. Cynthia leant forward and whispered encouragement; the animal put forward her last reserves of energy, and Cynthia steered her diagonally towards the far bank, so that some of the current's force might be behind her. They reached land a bare six paces from the deadly drop of the weir, which bellowed angrily at its escaped victim as Cynthia dragged Dick on to the bank, half dead.

For three minutes he lay without sign of life, while Cynthia worked his arms, as she had once seen an old sailor do, to pump the river out of him. When he began to revive she made him drink some cordial, which she carried in her clothes against the mischances of hunting. But it was not so much her ministrations as an unquenchable spirit within himself that, after an hour, brought him to his feet. His unquenchable spirit—and the necessity to prove his suspicions. "I must make sure, I must make sure," he muttered. His eyes were glittering and hard as diamonds: they frightened Cynthia.

CYNTHIA RESCUES DICK.

"Dick, sweet Dick, look not at me so. Basilisks sit in thine eyes. Why, thou lookest like a ghost, a murdered ghost," she whispered.

"Nay, my dear deliverer, no ghost am I, though murder's breath hath scorched my cheeks," he replied. Then, seeing her dismayed by his wild words, he took her hands, saying:

"Cynthia, thou must trust me yet a little: soon enough, I fear, all will be made plain. It may be that soon I will have to leave thee. Thou hast saved my life: but an thou wert to ask for it again, I would joyfully lay it down for thee. I love thee true, and will never forget thee wheresoever my adverse star may drive me."

He had quite forgotten that, by obeying his instinct in riding first over the bridge, he had saved her life too, though she might never know it. It did not matter, for she returned him a look that he was to remember a thousand times thereafter, when seas lay between them, and bring out of his memory as a miser brings out his choicest treasure. But for the moment nothing more was said, or needed to be said. Dick flung into the river the spoiled cloak that Cynthia had taken off him to pillow his head. Then he mounted her horse, took her up behind him, and pricked rapidly towards the castle, his clothes still damp upon him.

The sun's heat had brought mist out of the waterlogged ground. A rank steam rose up, clouding the castle walls as they approached. But the fire of anger within Dick seemed to keep the chill out of his bones: he rode with a single purpose, oblivious of Cynthia's arms sweetly belting his waist. At the wood's edge he dismounted, lifted her down. He was a leader now. She followed him to the ruined cottage, where he knelt by the wall and fumbled at a thick slab of masonry. Soon he hit upon the secret spring, and a section of wall at the bottom slid aside. A blackness yawned at them; they entered. Blackness deeper and more foul awaited them at the other end. As they drew near to the door of Sir Giles' room, Dick whispered to Cynthia to tread yet more warily. She obeyed him, with a new unquestioning submissiveness that was pleasing to both, though neither consciously noticed it.

Dick put his ear cautiously to the door, motioning the girl to do the same. Someone stirred within : there was the creak of a stool. Then silence again, disturbed only by the faintest sound, as of a man whistling between his teeth, the monstrous breathing of Stephen Sant. Suddenly a voice spoke, a familiar voice, yet with so dire an alteration of tone that Cynthia clutched Dick's hand convulsively as she recognized it.

" We should have news of the—of the happy event ere long, methinks."

" Aye, my haughty lady shall bring back the glad tidings : it will irk me not to see her scornful eyes beslubbered with tears. Sure, she doteth on the young whelp."

" But, Stephen, canst be certain that they will not both participate in this happy event of thine?"

" The bridge is narrow : two may not ride abreast : the gentleman will, of his pretty courtesy, lead the way over, and hey presto—it is over with him !" A rasping laugh.

" 'Tis well. I should profit naught by the girl's death; and she hath her uses here. Moreover, two corpses might conjure up suspicion, whereas one shall but draw down compassion for the sorrowing relatives."

A demon's chuckle followed the last remark. Then all was silent within for a space.

" Horrible, horrible !" whispered Cynthia, holding tight

to Dick; "that he, my uncle, should so—— Faugh, the cold, cunning, cowardly devil!"

Horrible it was; as though one should overhear a conference of the arch-demons of hell. Sant's voice was chill and toneless: it struck on Dick's ears like the voices of people talking when one is just falling asleep, disembodied, unnaturally loud. But the other voice, his cousin's, it curdled his blood like a poison: hate, malice, cruelty seemed to bubble up through his words, as baneful herbs seething in a witch's brew. It spoke again.

"It grows late. Why does the girl not return? Thou didst bungle twice, and I forgave thee. But by Heaven, if thou hast bungled this time, look not for mercy here. I will——"

The lisping voice lowered so that the listeners could not catch his words. Only a shuddering gasp from Sant informed them of its purport.

"Nay, master, nay! I have served thee faithfully ever. There is no botching this time. The planks were sawn through and but a hair of wood left."

Dick was stunned by these last proofs of his suspicions. His mind's eye saw the two faces within the room, leaning devilishly together in the flickering firelight, the leper-face of Sant and the vulture-face of Sir Giles. The vision turned his limbs to stone. It was Cynthia now who took the lead. Her quick brain had been hard at work. She led Dick, still all unnerved, back through the tunnel and out into the healthy daylight. Her plan was made.

"Dick, thou must flee this instant. There is not a moment to be lost, for soon they will send out to search for us."

"Flee? Rather will I return and confront the villain with his villainies."

"Nay, Dick, that were madness. Thou art no match

for my uncle and Stephen. They would deny all, and fashion some yet subtler means to end thee. If thou fleest at once, they will find thy cloak perchance in the river and suppose thee dead, and their hate will pursue thee no more."

"But what of thee, my brave Cynthia? Thou canst not remain with that monster."

"Thou needst not fear for me. Thou heardest; my uncle can come to no profit by my death. I will feign to have seen thee drowned before mine eyes. Methinks there will need little counterfeit of grief since thou and I are to be parted, though it is not death that comes between us. But hurry, Dick. Oh, hurry! Where wilt thou go?"

Resolution had been forming in Dick's mind. Since he must leave Cynthia, there was only one other friend to whom he could turn. He determined to make his way to Southampton and enquire after the whereabouts of Martin. If he was still at sea, he would try to find some means of returning to Dorset and put himself under the protection of Sir Herbert. But the sea called to him. He would take ship, perhaps win glory and wealth, and come back to claim his estates and Cynthia.

They clung together and kissed.

"I will come back, Cynthia."

"And I shall be waiting for thee, Dick."

Then she turned, drooping, and led her horse towards the castle and the forlorn years that were before her, and Dick set out through the woods southward.

PART THREE
THE SPANISH MAIN

CHAPTER XIII

LATE on the second day after leaving Clifford Castle, Dick trudged wearily under the stout tower gateway of Southampton. The little money he had had with him was all but spent on the food he had needed on the way, and he had not been able to afford the hire of a horse. No arm had reached out after him from the castle; Cynthia must have played her part well and left no doubts of his death. But the arm of the law had tried to snatch him : two village constables, seeing the lad in his travel-stained clothes, imagined him to be a beggar and raised hue and cry after him. For Dick had not the badge which Elizabeth's poor laws ordained that all licensed vagrants should wear. Had he been caught, he must inevitably have been haled back to the parish from which he came. The knowledge of this winged his weary heels, and he easily outdistanced the portly, puffing constables.

Later he had fallen in with a wandering company of gypsies, a hundred or more strong : one of those bands that moved slowly through the country like a cloud of locusts, scouts thrown out in front, stripping bare their line of march of anything they were allowed to pilfer. These folk took kindly to Dick and saved him from further pursuit, for he passed through several villages unnoticed in the swarm. Outside the walls of Southampton he said good-bye to the gypsies and, entering the town, enquired for the Rose tavern.

Down a maze of alleys he went, the last gleam of sunset gilding their squalid walls, with the tang of the sea ever stronger in his nostrils. Now he emerged on to the sea front and saw the sign of the Rose on his left. As he approached its door, a body sailed out and flopped into the gutter at his feet. The body was closely followed by a pair of dice and a roaring gale of a voice:

"Ha, thou son of mischief! Said I not the dice were cogged? Begone, and a hundred of lice go with thee!"

The body collected its sprawling members and resolved itself into a black-avised ruffian, who paused but to shake his fist at the doorway and slunk off. Dick's heart was so refreshed by the sound of that familiar voice that he forgot all his weariness and ran helter-skelter through the doorway into the arms of Martin. Difficult it would be to say whose was the greater surprise—Martin's at the boy's bolt-from-the-blue appearance, or Dick's at his amazing luck in finding Martin, who he had expected to hear was still at sea. He clung to Martin's oak-like body, half laughing, half sobbing: the mariner, seeing him to be overwrought and famished, took him inside and would neither ask nor answer questions till the boy was well victualled with beef, bread, and ale. Dick then related to him the events which had led to his hurried departure from the castle. As he unfolded Sir Giles' evil designs, Martin rumbled volcanically, ever and anon erupting with fiery oaths and threats of what he should do "had he the traitor's skinny gizzard between his hands." At one point he could scarcely be restrained from marching straightway upon the castle and hanging its occupants from the battlements. And when the tale was over he pondered for some time whether to be blown from the mouth of a gun or to be flayed alive and fastened to an ant-hill was the more fitting end for Sir Giles. Dick replied laughingly that revenge could wait till he had returned from sea and claimed his estate.

"Hold hard a minute, bully Dick," exclaimed the shrewd mariner; "thou sayest this Sir Giles hath good cause to presume thee dead?"

"Marry, he hath——"

"Then what is to prevent him claiming the estate at once? Meseems thou hast done his business as well for him as if thou wert indeed lying on the river-bed."

Dick was flabbergasted. Strange as it may seem, he had entirely failed to envisage this possibility: the stressful emotions of that last evening at the castle had blinded him: the complications of Cynthia's plan for his escape had concealed the obvious flaw in it. However, it was better to lose land than life. Besides, it was possible that, if Sir Giles immediately pressed his title to the estates, Cynthia might threaten to reveal the real happenings at Clifford, though such a course would be dangerous in the highest degree for one in her unprotected position, whether her story should be believed or no. At any rate, even if Sir Giles did come into possession of Willoughby Hall, Dick reasoned that on his return he could put the whole affair before Sir Francis Walsingham and by his patronage win it back from the usurper.

For the present he could feel no overmastering desire to fight for his heritage on land. His other heritage was beckoning to him in the swaying masts of ships and the sea that smiled mysteriously through the open window. With Martin by his side, and Cynthia in his heart, he felt eager for adventure. He asked Martin how he came to be back at Southampton so providentially.

"'Tis a short tale, and inglorious. I took ship a week after I left thee. But our consorts were parted from us in a great storm, and we were compelled to put in at the Indies and winter there, for the scurvy was working great scathe amongst our crew. Early in the new year, seeing that we stayed there to no purpose, our consorts not appearing at the rendezvous, we worked the ship short-handed back to England. We have refitted, and even now

our captain, Roger Trevaskis, prepareth to set out again.
We leave in two days."

"Thou wilt take me with thee, Martin?"

The sailor's eyes twinkled.

"Since thou art set on it. I warrant Roger Trevaskis
will not refuse Sir Richard Willoughby's son, though he
should have to jettison his best piece of ordnance to make
room for thee. To-morrow I will take thee to him."

Martin was as good as his word. Early in the morning
they threaded their way across the humming wharves, and
boarded the *Retribution*. Going aft they knocked at the
captain's door. A deep voice bade them enter. While
Martin was explaining his errand, Dick took stock of the
man under whom he hoped to serve. Roger Trevaskis was
thick-set and swarthy: his eyes were dark and brooding
as the uplands of his county Cornwall; these and his
black bushy beard and golden ear-rings gave him a
foreign look to Dick's eyes. He was harsh of speech, spar-
ing of gesture. Dick recalled what Martin had said of
him. His brother had been tortured to death by the
Inquisition and Roger had never forgotten it; for
every moment that his brother had suffered under the
Inquisitors he had vowed to slay ten Spaniards. If he
could take their gold too, well and good: but it was their
lives he thirsted for. Because of this, fortune-seekers were
sometimes chary of sailing with him. He played a lone
hand, and certain of his exploits had been frowned on by
the Queen. He had never been known to laugh, and but
once seen to smile—when a gun trained by his own hand
had hit the powder magazine of a galleon and blown
every soul in it into the sea, or the next world.

This rather forbidding figure now turned to Dick:

"So thou art Richard Willoughby's son. He was a
brave man. If thou art as like him in soul as thou art in

feature, I shall have no cause to repent of taking thee with me. Nay," he continued, as Dick began to stammer out his gratitude, " 'tis in deeds not in words thou must repay. And mark me, though thou art never so much thy father's son, I have no favourites on board my ship. Gentleman must pull on a rope and man a gun with common sailor. So my old admiral Francis Drake orders it, and so I order it. Thou seekest adventure, doubtless. Shalt have thy bellyful. But I promise no Eldorados; only hard working and hard fighting."

The curtness of his speech was softened by the honest grip of his hand: and Dick went ashore with Martin to buy equipment for the voyage, his heart well satisfied. On their return to the inn, they heard voices proceeding from the tap-room: Ned Taylor, the landlord, was conversing with a stranger. But no stranger, after all; the fat back, the rich wheezing voice—they could belong to none other than the good clerk, Master Rudgeley. Dick was overjoyed to meet his old tutor again, and soon they were sitting round a broiled ham, and Master Rudgeley was alternately engulfing vast slices of the delicacy and telling them his story.

On taking Dick into his own house Sir Giles had dispensed with the tutor's services. His occupation gone, he had applied to Sir Herbert, who had given him an introduction to a kinsman of his dwelling in the adjoining county. Rudgeley had acted as chaplain to this nobleman for nearly a year, when the latter dying and distant relatives coming into his estate who had no use for the chaplain's services, Rudgeley had again been cast adrift. The poor clerk was even now on his way to solicit the patronage of another great family; but, passing through Southampton, he had chanced to hear report of Dick's adventure, and had determined to meet his old pupil again

before seeking his fortunes elsewhere. He seemed very dis-
heartened by the ill-luck which had dogged him, and
Martin to raise his spirits said jestingly:

"Why, thou hadst better sail with us. I warrant we
shall need ballast when we strike the open sea."

To their surprise Rudgeley took this suggestion quite
seriously and besought Martin to find him employment
on the *Retribution*.

"Perchance thy captain standeth in need of a chaplain:
a-many souls must be in jeopardy where death's arrows
fly so thick."

Martin burst out in a roar of laughter.

"Chaplain, quotha! Nay, we carry no such commodi-
ties on shipboard. Little leisure have we for prayers betwixt storm and shot."

Then, seeing a hurt look in the clerk's face, he continued:

"Nay, mistake me not. I hold thy profession in no
disesteem. 'Tis but that I can promise thee no more than
a common sailor's duties and maybe a sniff at Spanish
doubloons if thou wouldst join us."

Beneath Rudgeley's commonplace exterior there lay a
romantic heart that was ever wont to beat more quickly
when he read of the glittering deeds of old, the warfare
beneath Troy's walls and the storm-fretted wanderings of
Odysseus. The sun that even now laid a golden pathway
across the waves into the heroic west inspired him to a
decision he might well have shrunk from in a less infectious environment. He sprang up, seized Martin's hand,
and demanded to be taken to Roger Trevaskis instanter.

"Well spoken, my bully clerk. Shalt have thy heart's
desire, or Martin will never more light linstock," cried
the jovial sailor, smiting Rudgeley so violently between
the shoulder-blades that he was precipitated on to the table

and his face buried in the wreckage of the ham. They went out and presently returned, the clerk beaming like a harvest moon, to announce that the captain, who was still short of men, had signed him on as a younker, or ordinary seaman. Dick was to be under Martin's special charge and berth with the rest of the gun crews on the gun-deck.

The morrow dawned fair, with a nipping south-easterly wind. Standing in the waist of the ship Dick watched the mole slip past and the *Retribution's* two smaller sister ships, the *Ark* and the *Mary of Lyme*, come nosing out of harbour behind them. It was Sunday, the mariners' lucky day for starting a voyage. But the chiming bells of the town were soon drowned by the creak of cordage, the slatting of sails, the shrill whistles of the quartermasters, and the smash and smother as the beak at the vessel's bows began to take the weight of the channel chop. England receded. Dick's heart leapt with the leaping ship: and somewhere, miles away on their starboard beam, Cynthia was riding the desolate woodlands, alone.

CHAPTER XIV

Dick soon adapted himself to the routine on shipboard and had leisure to take in the details of his new surroundings. The *Retribution* was a vessel of some 600 tons, smaller than the great ships of the Queen's navy, but larger than ordinary English merchantmen. She had three masts and the high decorated poop of the ships of that day: the weight of the poop caused her to pitch badly in a sea-way, in spite of the beak which was intended to counteract this motion. Often during the first days did Dick find his old tutor prone upon the deck, his face green as a cheese, calling upon death to deliver him from his anguish. And loud was the mirth of the ship's company when Rudgeley was sent aloft into the main-top, his belly quivering with terror as he clung to the shrouds.

But even he " suffered a sea-change." The waves ceased to harass his vitals: the spare diet curbed an appetite which wind and sun increased, and his figure was gradually reduced to reasonable dimensions. He became something of a favourite, too, with the crew: rough fellows to whom his ready wit appealed and who believed him a prodigy of learning. Dick was in his element now. His father's spirit seemed to blow through him with the trumpeting winds; and his whole body thrilled to the vital movements of the ship. Even the monotony of that confined life could scarcely repress his ardour. And deadly monotony it was. The pulse of the Atlantic swell upon the bows was like a clock, ticking slowly away, minute after minute, day after day. Nothing to be seen but the grey walls of wave, the grey towering sky, and the two ships behind them that soared and swooped from wave to wave like following gulls.

Dick soon learnt, too, the iron discipline which bound the crew together against the influence of savage sea and and sky. The ship's boys were often whipped by the boatswain for misdemeanours: some old sailors, indeed, believed that they would be baulked of a fair wind unless the boys were regularly whipped on a Monday morning. But Roger Trevaskis allowed no punishments that had not been earned, so Dick escaped this weekly affliction. Men who were detected lying were put for seven days under the charge of the Swabber, who gave them all the filthiest work about the ship to do. These penalties, however, meant little to sailors for whom pain and dirt were familiar experience.

There were other punishments, though, of a very different quality. After they had been some three weeks at sea, being delayed by constant head-winds, rations were reduced to " six upon four," which meant that six men must eat the allowance of but four. This was a commonplace of long-distance voyaging, and entailed little hardship if the provision was in good condition: which, owing to the mean rascality of the contractors, was often far from being the case. Where food was a commodity worth far more than its weight in gold, any sharp practice over the provisions was a capital crime.

One morning a buzz of anger arose in the forecastle, and presently a knot of men appeared dragging with them one of the pursers, an undersized, pimply creature in the last extremities of fear. He was haled on to the poop, where the captain and his lieutenant already stood, armed; for that angry buzz too often preluded mutiny. The spokesman stepped forward and charged the purser with having stinted his mess of their full ration and withheld the residue for himself.

" 'Tis a lie, a base lie!" frantically cried the culprit.

"Your proofs?" said Trevaskis shortly.

These were brought forward, and the purser's guilt proved beyond question.

"You know my punishment for pilfering. Boatswain, have this man keelhauled."

The wretch gave vent to such frightful screams on hearing these words that some of the crew began to mutter and eye each other askance, and Sim Cooper, the lieutenant, ventured to suggest to the captain that it were wiser to temper justice with mercy. Trevaskis looked at him steadily under his beetling brows, barked out: "You have heard my orders," and retired to his cabin. Cooper shot a surly glance at the retreating back, shrugged his shoulders ostentatiously, and ordered the ship to be brought up into the wind.

Dick watched the preparation for the punishment with a sick feeling at the pit of his stomach. A long rope was passed under the ship and the purser was fastened securely to it on the starboard side. Those holding the rope on the port side now slowly began to pull, while another gang holding the starboard coils released them through their fingers, keeping the rope taut. The man's face, twisted with terror, disappeared over the bulwarks. The boatswain gave the time for each haul upon the rope. After what seemed to Dick a life-time of waiting, the purser's huddled body appeared over the port bulwarks. He was insensible, three-quarters drowned. His body, as they lowered it to the deck, was a sickening spectacle: the clothes torn to ribbons and bloody strips of flesh raked from it by the barnacles on the ship's bottom.

Dick was so appalled by this savage punishment that he questioned Martin in the evening whether it was not too severe for the crime.

"Certes, 'tis no sight for young eyes," the gunner said,

"but bethink you, Dick. On such an ocean voyage the lives of nigh five hundred men hang on two threads, the chancy winds and the victuals. One day's stock of provision may mean the difference betwixt life and death for more than one poor sailor. So he that stealeth as much—though it be but a few weevilly biscuits and a gallon of sour beer—is in danger of becoming a wilful murderer."

Dick was soon to be convinced that there was justice—though it was rough justice—in this point of view. For some days after the event the winds held fair and the ships rollicked merrily on their way into warmer latitudes. But one morning he came on deck for his watch to find the streamers at the yard-arms drooping lifeless and no white furrow trailing astern. The sun climbed wearily over the heavens, glaring down without pity upon the blue sea, that reflected back its rays as pitilessly. The pitch in the deck-seams grew sticky, and the crew gathered under awnings and wherever there was shade, like desert travellers sheltering in oasis. A sluggish swell pushed at the ship, imperceptibly eating away the men's nerve with the incessant slapping of sails and the uneasy wrenching of the guns at their moorings.

Now the heat began to take effect upon the provisions as well as the souls aboard. Food was found rotting and drink brackish. The spectre of famine hove up in the offing, drawing ever closer as the days passed without a flaw of wind. Quarter rations were ordered. Often would the master and the lieutenant be seen on the poop, anxiously calculating their position with astrolabe, quadrant, back-staff and cross-staff. Men dragged themselves wearily about their duties, whistling between parched lips for a wind that never came, or squatted in groups bickering over dice and knucklebones. Heat and inaction bred a poison in their veins, so that they ripened for mischief.

Every day Roger Trevaskis ordered the great 30-foot long boat that usually towed astern to be manned by successive shifts and drag the ship forward: not so much for the mile or so they gained thereby as to exhaust the men's physical powers and so reduce the chances of private quarrel or mutiny. Trevaskis possessed that prime quality of the natural leader, the ability to gauge the temper of the men under him and so judge the exact moment for action of any sort. And the men's tempers smouldered within them like combustible goods in a ship's hold, ready to burst into open conflagration.

But their blind, smouldering resentment was to be quenched ere it burst heart's hatches. The eighth day since the beginning of the calm was even more intolerably airless than the previous seven. The sun glowed a hectic copper-red, as though in the last stages of some feverish disease, and the men sweated and panted in sympathy. As the day wore on clouds began to bank up in the north-west, their purple ranks returning the angry look of the sun. As they increased, so did the unnatural silence of sea and sky: the whole hemisphere seemed to be holding its breath, waiting for some shattering event.

Roger Trevaskis ordered the lee ports to be closed: for there was the danger, if this was left till the storm broke, of the first assault of wind heeling the vessel over so that these ports were forced under water and she foundered. The bonnets of all the sails were taken off and only the courses, a small expanse of canvas, remained, reefing of sails being unknown in these days. A second quarter-master was sent to reinforce the one at the helm: high on the poop stood the captain, incessantly watching the omens of the west; the less experienced members of the crew gathered in uneasy groups, while even the mariners —the oldest sailors—tapped out their pipes and cleared

their hearts for action. Dick had been busy with the
master gunner's gang on the gun-deck, fastening the
ordnance with double lashings against the imminent
storm.

This task over, he went up into the waist. A terrible
spectacle presented itself to him as he looked out over the
weather beam. The whole sky seemed to hang toppling
over the fleet in tier upon tier of sultry cloud. A breath
or two of wind, skirmishers of the tempest, fluttered the
streamers. Then a stronger breath came, and it was as
though it had puffed out the light: for gloom descended
swiftly as a drop curtain, through which could be dimly
descried a black line running at them across the sea.

"The squall! The squall!" a hundred throats shouted.
The sail trimmers stood to their posts in the waist, and
Dick had just time to see, ere he ran below, a horizon-
broad line of wave leaping towards the ship, baring its
white teeth. As he emerged into the darkness of the gun-
deck, for the heavy square ports were now closed, this
wave seized the ship and flung her over upon her side.
Over and over she went, trembling at the onset of the
ravenous pack of waves that each leapt higher above her
as though to press home the advantage which the first had
gained.

With the waves came their ally, the wind, stunning the
crew with thunderous claps of sound and pushing like a
remorseless hand at the strips of sail. Trevaskis leapt to
the kicking helm and aided the quartermasters to bring
the ship up into the wind. The waist was a boiling cauldron of water, and two of the trimmers had already been
tossed over the side, their screams drowned in the maniac
laughter of the storm and the hissing of mast-high spray.
Through the smother could be seen ever and anon, though
no one had leisure to look, the dark shapes of the *Ark*

THE GUN BREAKS ADRIFT.

and the *Mary of Lyme* bobbing distractedly upon the
frenzied sea; slowly, while men bit their lips or mumbled
oaths or Paternosters according to their disposition, the
Retribution righted herself and wearily as a beast at bay
turned to face the tempest. You could almost hear above
the din the sigh of relief that rose up from five hundred
hearts.

The ship gathered way and battled bravely against the
elements, but for every foot she gained towards her viewless goal she was driven yards to leeward. Fortunately the
storm had taken her in the open sea and there was no
lee-shore waiting to crunch her timbers into fragments.
Meanwhile the guns' crews awaited below the fortunes of
the struggle that was being waged overhead. Suddenly
the confused din of thumping seas and groaning tackle
was pierced by a report loud as a pistol shot, followed by
a few rending sounds and then a sinister rumble. A 30-
pounder demi-cannon, one of a battery of three, the big-
gest guns on the ship, had broken loose. Backward and
forward it ran, like a maddened bull trying to escape its
tormentors. The crews ran forward to chain up the monster, and one man, thrust underneath it by the press, had
his leg snapped by its iron wheels before Martin could
bark out his orders, and the rest drew back, leaving Martin
himself and five others to carry on the struggle.

These now hurled themselves upon the gun and gripped
the broken tackle. But just at that moment a great sea
canted the vessel over and the cannon, lumbering forward
and dragging the men with it, rammed the ship's side.
Water began to trickle through, then to spurt in jets. The
timbers had been started. Luckily the leak was above the
waterline and on the windward side, so that it did not lie
below the surface for more than a few moments at a time.
The gun recoiled again. A sailor ran to the leak with

canvas and oakum, and Martin rapidly spliced the frayed ropes' ends to new ropes that had been inserted in the floor-bolts. But the blind rage of the gun claimed one more victim. It thundered forward once again. Martin yelled a warning as the ropes were torn through his bleeding hands. Too late. Dick, palsied as by a nightmare, saw the deadly muzzle rush at the sailor who was mending the leak, and pin him screaming to the side, his spine shattered.

As though exhausted by its murderous work, the cannon now stood still and allowed itself to be securely lashed. That scene of bull-baiting, played out on the dark stage of the gun-deck to the accompaniment of the storm's pandemonium, stuck in Dick's memory to his dying day. But for the present there could be no leisure for brooding upon it. Hour after hour the unleashed devils of wave and wind tormented the ship. For a night and a day and a night there was no breathing space for anyone on board. Only on the second morning did there come a perceptible abatement of the storm's force. Gradually the wind went down: then, turning with their luck, backed round so that it blew from the north-east and pushed them along on their course. The sun, too, returned, in sobered mood, and shone mildly upon the ship that drove its eager prow deep into the sea. Only the waves stayed hostile, heaving sullenly like the ribs of a panting, implacable monster, so that the vessel see-sawed dizzily from height to depth. But even they in the end were soothed, and one morning the *Retribution* glided into the island rendezvous, sorely battered, her consorts lost to sight, her long-boat snatched away by the storm; yet joyous somehow and triumphantly tranquil she looked, as one who has fought a good fight.

CHAPTER XV

FOR several days they lay at their anchorage in the Bermudas, awaiting the arrival of their sister ships, and recruiting their strength with the fresh water and the fruits of the bounteous island. Hearty was the activity on board as new sails were bent and the storm's damage made good: the men wandering in relays through the coloured forest could hear afar the tapping of their comrades' hammers; and if they climbed to an eminence they could see the look-outs, high in the tops of the embayed vessel, peering into the flawless horizon as into a crystal for tidings of the *Ark* and the *Mary of Lyme*.

Dick took the first opportunity of going ashore with a landing party, anxious to see the sights of the island paradise. Strange it felt to be on solid ground once more: for some minutes it seemed to rock and sway beneath his feet accustomed to the perpetual motion of the ship. Their tasks of filling the water-casks and storing the boat's lockers with breadfruit and melons were soon over, and the men separated into groups to explore the fringes of the interior. The jungle before they entered it seemed dark and soundless; but once under its exuberant leafage they found the gloom lit up with the motley flashings of parrots and vivid with the pipings and squeaks and rustle of a thousand creatures. It was like a tapestry come alive, thought Dick: and as he thought, his mind wandered back into the great draughty rooms of Clifford Castle, where faded arras stirred restlessly upon the walls. And he wondered what Cynthia was doing now and whether she was indeed as safe from the malevolence of Sir Giles as she had professed. Shame took him that he could so have left her, that he could have forgotten her so often in the crowded life of shipboard.

Deep in his memories he lagged behind his companions, scarcely conscious of the good-humoured sallies they made over their shoulders.

"Come apace, Dick," one cried, "or thou wilt find thyself anon in the belly of a tiger."

"Nay, let him be, the poor mome," returned another; "he hath eaten a surfeit of melons and doth but tarry till we are out of sight to tickle his throat and be rid on't."

"Or perchance he hath the green-sickness and pineth for his piggesnie in England."

Their voices receded and were snuffed out in the darkness ahead. Dick still walked on dreaming. Suddenly, looking up, he saw a gorgeous butterfly, crimson and orange, flittering across the track. He whooped and sprang into the thickets after it, snatching off his cap to net the prize. A pretty dance it led him, on and on through the jungle's heart, forgetful of all but the brilliant will-o'-the wisp that jigged in the air before him. He gave it up, and sat down panting on a fallen trunk. Then, breath restored, turned to put himself again on the track he had left. Five minutes he walked, ten minutes, fifteen, his pace imperceptibly quickening as still no track came in sight.

Now panic pounced on him out of the shades. He was lost. Nothing mattered but to run, to get out of this rich cloying darkness. On and on he stumbled, his feet tripped by creepers and sucked at by patches of marsh, his small sobbing cries mocked by the monkeys overhead. Then reason returned. He cursed himself for losing his nerve like a child. What would his father, or Cynthia, think of it? His companions could not be far. He took some deep breaths, then shouted. No answer. He shouted again. His

voice was blanketed by the gross vegetation. No use. A
new idea struck him. If he listened hard he would hear
the sounds of the men at work upon the ship, and could
steer his course by that. . . . It was no good. High noon
overhead, they were all resting sheltered from the torrid
heat. It occurred to him that if he could climb a tree he
would be able to see the bay or at any rate the position of
the sun, whose light was at present diffused by the filter-
ing leaves.

He found a tree that gave promise of foothold and
climbed swiftly up, the monkeys gibbering at him as they
fled. He reached the top. Nothing to be seen but layer
after layer of sullen green. The tree was in a hollow. But
looking down his heart leapt to descry through the leaves
a track, which, if he had walked on a score more paces,
he must inevitably have found. Which way should he
take, though; up the track or down? At any rate, it was
bound to lead somewhere, and he was on the point of
descending when he heard a murmur of voices to the
right. His mouth was open to give a hail, when that sixth
sense of his spoke a warning. Why should men talk in
those furtive whispers in the depth of a forest where none
could possibly be listening? He held his peace and
stretched sight and hearing to pierce the muffled gloom.

"I could swear I heard shouts coming from this direction but a few minutes past."

"Nay, thou art deceived. The island is full of noises."
The speakers came into view round a bend of the path.
To Dick's amazement they proved to be the lieutenant,
Sim Cooper, and Dodson, the purser who had been keelhauled. Close upon their heels stepped one of the quartermasters, Black Thomas, a powerful bull-necked fellow,
whose head was bent forward as though in secret conclave
with the others. A curiously assorted trio to be taking the

air together in the heart of a forest, Dick thought. As they came level with the tree where Dick was hiding the lieutenant spoke again, still in the same secretive tones.

"The hour is not yet come. But come it will, and that soon. Be patient, and dark as the grave. How, my bullies, have we sailed a thousand miles to return empty-handed? What say ye?"

"Nay, by cock!" growled the quartermaster.

"Nay!" piped the reedy voice of the purser.

"Remember, the word is 'gold or gizzard.' When ye hear that, stand to't. Ye know what needs be done," the lieutenant continued, his words growing fainter as they receded. "Whom say ye now we have with us?" The voices blurred into unintelligible sounds; and Dick, after a decent interval, descended from his tree and struck on to the path in the direction taken by the speakers. Sorely puzzled he was by what he had heard. No tangible ground for suspicion in their talk; yet the manner of it— that was strange indeed. Racking his brains to discover some meaning behind these veiled utterances, he found himself stepping out of the forest, the shore and the boat's crew a hundred yards in front, apparently waiting for him.

A hail of chaff fell upon him as he drew near, but it was soon silenced by the lieutenant, who stepped forward, his angular body stooping towards the boy, and with an intent look said to him:

"Hast tarried long, young cub. Didst lose thyself without thy dam? Was it not thy voice we heard calling for help, ha?"

Some animal sense warned Dick that he was on the verge of a trap. He became conscious that he disliked the lieutenant, his bullying voice, his swivel eye, the thin lips and the nose that swelled to an unpleasing bluntness at the tip. He answered:

"No, sir: I was not lost nor did I call for help. I crave thy pardon for my tardiness. I heard not the signal of recall."

Sim Cooper showed signs of desiring to continue the catechism. But suddenly everyone's attention was diverted by a loud cry from the ship's mastheads, followed soon by a crashing cannonade from her sides: its echoes had scarcely died away when a faint answering boom came out of the horizon. The *Ark* and the *Mary of Lyme* had made their landfall and were returning the salute.

In the excitement of reunion and the days of feverish activity that followed, for the two ships had been terribly battered by the storm and all hands were set to work on the task of repair, Dick had little space to reflect upon the curious incident in the forest. And he might well have let it pass out of mind altogether but for the lieutenant's eye, which he observed from time to time fixed in a meditative way upon him. This scrutiny made him so uncomfortable that he took the opportunity, the first day the fleet put to sea, of imparting what he had heard to Martin. Scarcely was the story out of his mouth when Martin took him, under cover of darkness, to the captain's cabin: where he was made to repeat it in minutest detail. When he had finished, Trevaskis tugged his beard and exchanged a meaning look with Martin; then turning to Dick said:

"Young sir, thy island escapade may yet put me in thy debt. Meanwhile, not a word of this to any soul. But whenever thou hearest 'gold or gizzard' spoken on this ship, bring me word of it on the instant. . . . 'Gold or gizzard,' forsooth," he continued, speaking half to himself, "what a farrago is this! Do they think themselves play-actors, ranting to the groundlings with lath sword on hip?"

Dick perceived that his presence was no longer desired,

so he returned to the gun-room; but it was some time before Martin followed him and with compressed lips and unwonted taciturnity that he slung his hammock and turned in.

The ships were soon sailing upon the Spanish Main, that adventurous stretch of sea which lay between the West Indies and the mainland. An atmosphere of tension prevailed on board, for they were in enemy waters and any time now there might be raised the sails of some treasure-laden convoy or single warship. Roger Trevaskis, who on the journey out had for the most part kept to his cabin, summoned out only by emergency, now trod the poop hour after hour snuffing the air like a veteran hound seeking the scent of its hereditary foe. Nothing, however, was sighted till, a week after leaving the Bermudas, they stood in nearer to shore and beheld a galliass tacking southward, hugging the coast. She appeared to be a vessel of about the same tonnage as the *Retribution*.

An order was barked, and the whole ship sprang into life. The officers and soldiers retired to don their armour: screens of painted cloth were raised above the bulwarks to hide those on deck from the enemy's fire: and the gun crews, stripped to the waist, ran in the guns and rammed home the charges—flannel-covered cartridge first, then a wad of rope-yarn, then the ball, then another wad to prevent the ball rolling out prematurely. Dick, with several of the strongest boys, was engaged in removing the shot from the racks along the side and piling it pyramid-wise beside the guns.

Peering out through a porthole when his task was done, he saw that the galliass was now foaming along at increased speed, a bank of oars reinforcing the billowy sails, and the *Retribution's* course was set to cut her off.

"Yarely, my hearties, yarely," Martin cried to his grim-

lipped men, " yon is a fine bird, but we shall wing her ere
sun sets : we shall ruffle her fine feathers; what say ye?"

A deep growl rose from their throats. Dick became
aware that his own was very dry and found himself yawn-
ing uncontrollably with apprehension. Martin, noticing
this, gave the boy a great slap on the back.

"Hey, my game-cock, shalt fire the first shot for luck.
Marry, what would not thy father have given to be on
deck now, a fair prize in sight and a fair breeze to carry
us upon her!"

His hearty words, his reminder of Sir Richard, were
just what Dick needed to fortify his heart, and he stood to
the demi-cannon with a clear head and a faint smile upon
his lips. He could hear the silver whistles of the quartermasters overhead, and very faintly a challenging trumpet
call from the Spanish ship. Martin peered along the
barrel, screwing up his eyes : then took the tobacco pipe
from his mouth and handed it to Dick.

"It were but polite to give the first word of greeting
to yon flouncing dame," he said, grinning broadly.

Dick leant over and tapped the glowing ashes into the
touch hole. A shattering roar. The piece recoiled savagely
and was checked by the breeching, a stout rope that
fastened the carriage to the ship's side. The ball bounced
once upon the intervening water, then cracked audibly
against the galliass' timbers, full amidship.

"A true shot, Dick," applauded the master gunner,
"but something short of a range. I had thought we were
at a thousand yards : but this plaguy sun doth so bedazzle
mine eyes."

For it was late afternoon and the Spaniard, in the
western berth, had the advantage of the light. Aware of
this, Roger Trevaskis laid his ship off several points to
starboard, so as to come up under the stern of the galliass

and give his gunners better visibility. The wily Spaniard, however, was not to be so easily caught. His sail-trimmers sprang into activity; the oarsmen on his port side backed water with a flurry of foam; and the ship swung round towards the *Retribution* and bore down upon her straight out of the sunset. Both vessels were now approaching each other at top speed; and the distance between them rapidly narrowing, Trevaskis brought the *Retribution* up into the wind so that Martin might give the enemy a full broadside.

"She seeketh to board us," exclaimed Martin, his clenched fist raised to the gunners who stood ready with smouldering match; "mayhap she will think twice of it with a load of iron in her guts."

And he lowered his hand. There was an ear-splitting crash as every demi-cannon, culverin and demi-culverin on the starboard side fired. The ship plunged like a restive horse at touch of whip. When the smoke curled away, a fearful havoc showed upon the galliass: her mizzen was gone by the board, and her timbers were scored in a dozen places by the passage of the English shot. A shout of jubilation arose from the *Retribution*, and a far louder one when a white flag was seen running up the enemy's halliards. Only Martin shook his head and said doubtfully:

"I like it not. Your Spaniard is a doughty fighter and yields not so easily if he hath aught to fight for. 'Tis either treachery or he hath nothing under hatches."

The English ship approached her disabled foe cautiously, every gun loaded. Trevaskis and a score of men, armed to the teeth, leapt into the long-boat and rowed to the galliass. Dick could see him on the deck now, in converse with the Spanish captain, who appeared to make deprecating gestures. Trevaskis spoke a word and turned curtly on his heel. Six of his men ran below, and the

Spanish crew began to hustle madly into their boats. The
long-boat returned and Trevaskis addressed his expectant
men.

"Lads, our labour is in vain. Yon galliass runneth light;
not a gold-bar aboard. I have scuttled her and bade the
crew save themselves. The Don said there was not room
for all his company in the boats, so I told him they must
e'en swim for it then."

The grim jest tickled the sailors' rough humour and
their resentment at having drawn a blank was temporarily
mollified. But there was whispering below decks that
night which boded no good unless some more solid recompense should soon attend them.

CHAPTER XVI

"Marry, I had better have stayed in England and starved among my books than turned hand to this murderous profession."

"Why, thou miscallest it indeed. War hath ever been an honourable trade. Thou canst not deem Drake or Hawkins—or my father, to be murderers?"

The speakers were Dick and Rudgeley. The latter had been one of the boat's crew that had boarded the galliass, and since their return his countenance had been strangely stripped of its usual easy joviality.

"An honourable trade? Aye, so it is reputed; and for some choice spirits it may be so. But, bethink you, for every man that draweth sword in honour's cause there be a hundred that fight only for avarice or of bloody-mindedness. Look about you on this ship. 'Tis gold, not glory, the men lust after: all save the captain, and his heart hath no room for aught but revenge. 'Twas not thus that my Master taught."

"I understand it not," replied Dick, sorely puzzled by such alien ideas; "man hath always fought man; the Church useth violence against infidels; and sovereigns delight to honour brave captains."

"Aye, so it is. But my heart misgiveth me to see blood shed."

"Why, thy heart misgave thee not," pursued Dick, "when thou didst embark upon this venture. Didst clamour then to be at the Spaniard."

"Thou sayest true. Battle is fair in prospect, but foul in act. When I climbed yon galliass' side and saw the execution of our guns, men dead or crying for death, the wastage of blood, I was sickened of my prating about victory and honour."

"Death cometh soon or late for all," returned Dick, repeating his father's words spoken that last Christmas morning they had been together; " surely 'tis noble in a man to face it bravely in the green summer of his life, nor shun its face till his limbs are too feeble to escape it?"

"Words, Dick, words!" said the tutor with a wry smile; " thou hast thy father's spirit, and battle was ever the breath of his nostrils. But I am timid, alas, and no fighting man. When I saw those decks running with blood, 'twas the sobbing of wives and orphaned children I heard, not the Nunc Dimittis of brave glory."

This struck home more forcibly upon Dick's mind than his old tutor's other arguments. His thought flew back to Cynthia, and he wondered if she still loved him and whether she would grieve if he did not return from sea. Rudgeley spoke again.

" 'Tis rumoured we sail for Santa Lucia, to ransack its treasures. Doubtless we shall bombard the town. There are women and children there. Why should they suffer for man's quarrel with man? If a man would sign articles with death, that is his own affair: but must he contract also to slay the innocent? I fear me I have no stomach for such business."

Santa Lucia was indeed their destination. The eyes of the crew glittered, gold and jewels were reflected in their savage concentration, as the ship drew nearer to the un-suspecting town. Was it unsuspecting, though? pondered Roger Trevaskis. Might not the captain of the scuttled galliass have conveyed word to its occupants of an English fleet in the vicinity? He was a fool not to have drowned them all with their vessel. Dead men tell no tales. And ten years, five years ago he would have thought nothing of doing so. Was he growing too old, was the edge of revenge growing blunt? The image of his tortured brother rose up spectrally in his mind; he swore under his breath and drove himself to plan the attack. But one thing must first be ascertained. Even if the Spaniards had no warning of their approach, there might be an armada lying in the harbour too numerous to be attacked with three ships. Trevaskis' experienced and practical mind had no use for foolhardiness. He decided to try and get wind of the enemy's strength.

So it was that the crew's appetite for plunder grew yet more ravenous through delay. For Trevaskis first put into land at dead of night twenty miles from the town, hoping to catch some Indian from whom the information might be extracted. And, this failing, he stood away just out of sight of Santa Lucia, and sailed up and down for several days in the expectation of falling in with some coasting vessel. But the sea seemed blank as the land; and while the *Retribution* and her consorts patrolled in vain, the patience of some was chafed almost through, while even the more level-headed began to wonder whether lightning assault had not been better policy than this cautious hesitation.

One night, the fourth of their to-and-fro cruising, Dick found the air on the gun-deck so sultry and oppressive that he could not sleep, so he decided to go above for a breather. Stepping quietly through the canvas-separated berths, so as not to wake the sleepers, he climbed the companion and put his head through the hatch. A tropic darkness shrouded mast and bulwark. Dick breathed gratefully the night-scented air. He was about to go below again when a tense whisper, almost at his elbow, breathed out of the blackness.

"Gold or gizzard! At dawn!"

"Aye, aye, sir," came the answer.

Then feet padded softly away; stopped; the whisper was repeated. It was the lieutenant's voice. Dick crept down the ladder, wakened Martin, and told what he had heard.

"The captain must have word of this. Go to him, Dick, and let none see thee in going."

As the boy ascended the ladder again, Martin went quietly through the berths, here and there shaking a man out of sleep and whispering certain instructions. In the meantime Dick was moving with infinite caution across the waist towards the poop. He had almost got there when he became aware that the darkness in front had grown more solid. Straining his eyes he perceived a group of men clustered about the ladder and the entrance to the captain's quarters. Roger Trevaskis was cut off from communication. Luckily the men had not seen Dick, and he retreated an inch at a time, scarce daring to breathe till he was under hatches again. A plan had already formed in his mind. He found Martin and muttered to him:

"The way is blocked. We must contrive another. Lower me a rope over the side."

Martin gripped the boy's hand and let the rope out through a square porthole. Dick wriggled through after it and swarmed down, lowering himself without a splash into the sea. Then he hauled himself along the ship's out-sloping side, praying that there might be no sharks wakeful in its vicinity. He reached the stern, clambered up the high carved face till he was standing on the stern-walk, and tapped quietly on the captain's outer door. In a trice it swung open and a pistol was levelled at Dick's head.

"Shoot not. 'Tis I, Dick Willoughby," he whispered. The pistol was lowered and Roger Trevaskis drew him into the cabin. In undertones, lest the picket on the poop should hear, he told his tale. Trevaskis patted his back.

DICK WARNS THE CAPTAIN.

"Thou hast done well. I shall not forget it. Martin is warned, thou sayest? Naught remaineth, then, but to await the dawn. These play-boy traitors shall find 'tis easier said than done to catch an old dog napping."

His face set for a moment grim as granite. Then he threw himself on his bed and was soon snoring as lustily as any farmer safe within a peaceful homestead. Dick was amazed at his iron nerve. He himself could not as much as close an eyelid, but sat up, all his muscles taut, and heard his own heart ticking out the interminable hours till dawn. After centuries, it seemed, had passed, he heard the tramping of feet as the watch was changed. Centuries more passed. A gleam appeared in the east, and presently the sun began to lift itself like a red-hot cannon ball out of the steaming waters.

At the same instant there was a thudding of feet and a buzzing snarl of voices; and Roger Trevaskis came wide awake, and, motioning Dick to follow him, walked steadily out on to the poop. A blur of faces, ghastly in the uncertain light, looked up at them from the waist. From various parts of the crowd, where the mutineers stood, growls of menace arose—"Slit his throat!" "Where is our gold?" "No more delay!" A voice at the back of the mob bellowed out a particularly lurid threat; Dick's spirits tumbled below zero: it was Martin's voice; he could see his red beard upthrust, his fist wildly brandished. Martin, too, a traitor? It could not be.

Now the whole company was being leavened by the malice of the mutineer ringleaders and seethed with confused sound and movement. Suddenly a dead silence fell. The lieutenant, Black Thomas, and two stalwart seamen mounted the poop ladder. Sim Cooper walked right up to Trevaskis, his arms folded, a sword in one hand. Trevaskis yielded not an inch, but stood with legs apart and hands behind back. The lieutenant spoke in a harsh, hectoring voice audible to every man on the ship.

"Captain, we have delayed long enough. We sail with thee to fill our purses, not to stravague up and down the sea. If thou likest not to lead to the attack, zoons, there be some less chicken-hearted among this company who will take thy place."

Mutters of approval spread like wild-fire through the crowd. Dick, looking up, noticed a movement at the back, but, before he could follow it, his attention was diverted to the group in front of him. Trevaskis, standing firm as a basalt rock, began to speak:

"So. Thou skulking fox! Thou thinkest to supplant me. A pretty leader thou'dst make, with thy play-acting ways, thy prattle of gold and gizzard, thou white-livered vermin. Thou art rotten and fit for nothing but treachery or the worms. We'll have no bad meat on this ship. Faugh! The very air about thee stinketh! If thou must poison aught, go poison the fishes!"

And with a movement so quick that the eyes of the onlookers could scarce follow it, while the infuriated lieutenant had hardly begun to unfold his arms to avenge the insults, Trevaskis seized his cadaverous figure, whirled it aloft and slung it straight into the sea. The ship heeled as every man jostled to the side. A fin slit the water; a white belly turned; and the white face of Sim Cooper was whisked below the surface. Nothing more of him was seen but a few streaks of blood curling on the oily sea.

The crew now broke up into uncertain groups, some applauding the captain's action, others demanding revenge. On the poop Black Thomas, who had been momentarily stunned by his leader's fate, started to life and with bloodshot eyes and slavering mouth sprang at Dick, roaring out:

"Thou misbegotten cub, 'tis thou hast betrayed us!"

Dick would most certainly have followed the lieutenant into the sea had not Roger Trevaskis, pivoting on his toes as Black Thomas lunged past him, smashed his rocky fist into the side of the man's head. He dropped as though the mainmast had fallen on him, and ere the gaping mouths of the crew could emit a gasp of astonishment, Trevaskis bounded to the edge of the poop and, pointing over their heads, cried:

"If there be any others who hanker to exchange blows, let them step forward. But 'tis iron hail-shot they shall feel now, not flesh and bone."

Like a flock of sheep turning to face some advancing danger, the men swivelled round head and eyes, not daring to move a foot. A windy sigh surged up from them. On the forecastle stood Martin and half a dozen loyal gunners, grinning along the muzzles of the quick-firing guns which pointed full at the mob in the waist. Trevaskis and Martin had laid their plans well. The captain now spoke again, his face almost black with pent-up rage.

"For two pins I'd have the pack of ye blown to perdition. Ye would dare question my authority, would ye? I am too faint-hearted to lead ye to the assault, am I? Very well, we attack Santa Lucia to-morrow, and your blood be on your heads if ye find a nest of hornets there and no treasure of gold. But we sail not a yard till justice is done and ye have hung up these mutinous dogs that would have seduced ye, as a warning to any others that may have treachery in their dirty veins. To it, my lads!"

A bloodthirsty baying went up from the fickle crew, and presently the *Retribution* was dipping westward towards Santa Lucia with six figures dangling and dancing from her yard-arms.

9

CHAPTER XVII

A GUSTY wind from the north slanted them speedily towards their objective. As soon as the haze of the land was seen lying dimly on the horizon, the fleet was hove to and the captains of the *Ark* and the *Mary of Lyme* came aboard the *Retribution* for a council of war. Roger Trevaskis allowed Dick the honour of waiting upon them in the cabin, and as he bustled to and fro with the wine and dishes of food, he heard snatches of conversation.

" We attack to-morrow morning. I shall bombard the forts at long range. Do you two bear up in support and engage any shipping that saileth out of harbour."

" Are there like to be galleys lying there?"

" Would to God I knew! I am not wont to be backward in assault, but these last days I have been uneasy."

" We would not gainsay thy fancy. Were it not better to push further south and attack elsewhere?"

" Nay, my crew groweth plaguy restive. I know not how much longer I can hold them. Ye have seen the proofs strung up on my yard-arms."

" Marry, 'tis a banner something strange to flaunt before the Spaniards."

" Galleys or no galleys, we follow thee to the death, Roger. Have no fear of that. Come, man, 'tis not like thee to be in the dumps when battle is toward."

Trevaskis heaved a sigh. " Aye, the war-dog is getting old for his work. Beshrew me, though, if we give not these murderous Dons some of their own entertainment to-morrow. Would that the winds were not so chancy. A steady breeze and we might sail circles round every galleon and galley on the seas. But these fickle winds that puff and swoon away fight for the Spaniards ever."

The council soon after dispersed. The crews caroused merrily, eager for action. The next morning, under the cover of the misty dawn, the fleet stood in stealthily towards Santa Lucia. As the sun rose behind them the lookouts could see its white houses and fringe of palms and two galleons lying at the quays. Dick, remembering Rudgeley's words, felt a momentary pang of revulsion. The town lay so white and innocent, a child asleep, that was soon to be battered and bruised and spoilt by merciless cannonade.

No such thought passed through the mind of Roger Trevaskis. He breathed a sigh of relief to find no dreaded galleys at anchor there. Let the winds do what they will now: it was a fair contest, sail against sail. Ant-like figures could be seen scurrying into the forts and aboard the galleons, and another train of figures—women, children, old men, Indians, they were—moving in the opposite direction, towards the hills beyond the town. Trevaskis sailed his ship to 1,300 yards range, then brought her up into the wind. The guns were loaded and run out already. It was a long shot. The forepart of the gun-carriages was raised with crowbars, and the quoins—graded wedges of wood—hammered in beneath to elevate the muzzles. Even as Martin's hand was about to fall, the signal for the broadside, the forts on either side of the harbour mouth winked with fire and an irregular booming sounded across the water, which soon was alive with jumps of spray where the enemy shot had fallen short. The reverberations had not died away when a thunder-clap roared from the English ship. Martin and his men had their eye in to-day. A cloud of dust floated up from the left-hand fort, and soon they could see cracks in its wall. Three more volleys and these cracks widened and the fort fell slowly apart like a house of cards.

By now the two galleons had hoisted sail; but they were slow to pass the harbour mouth,.for the wind, which was blowing but fitfully in the English sails, was the lightest of airs further inshore. The *Ark* and the *Mary of Lyme* took up position well forward of the *Retribution*, some hundred yards to port and starboard, and began firing at the outcoming galleons. Meanwhile the *Retribution* turned her attention to the other—and greater—fort. The Spaniards had the worse of the light this time; their shots, fired straight into the sun, scattered wildly over the sea. Some rigging cut and a man's head torn from his shoulders were all the casualties on board the *Retribution* for the first twenty minutes.

Her guns were firing by batteries now, and as each could fire only at five-minute intervals, Dick had plenty of leisure to look out through portholes and see how the fight was faring. He saw the galleons, nosing out of harbour, turn hard a-starboard and slip slowly southward with the wind behind them: whether in flight or to gain better visibility he could not tell. Flame spurted from the foremost galleon; there was a boom and a whistling in the air; then an appalling crash. A lucky shot had struck full into the muzzle of an English gun that had just been run out. A fountain of sparks as iron met iron. Then an explosion like the crack of doom. The impact had fired the charge and the gun burst, scattering jags of metal broadcast, killing or wounding every man in the battery.

Infuriated by this reverse, the rest of the gun's crews, stripped to the waist, their eyes rolling white in powder-blackened faces, redoubled their activity till the cannon were almost red-hot and an incessant hail of iron was pouring into the luckless fort. The sea about them was pocked and churned with shot, while a fog of dust from smitten masonry enveloped their objective. So thick was this that for several moments they did not see the white flag that had been run up above the fort.

Trevaskis at once conned his ship close under the lee of the *Ark*, and bade her captain stand in to the town and take their surrender, while the *Retribution* and the *Mary of Lyme* should follow the galleons: for he suspected that they might be trying to escape with full cargoes of treasure below hatches. At this point of the engagement Dick was sent on deck by Martin with a message to the captain. After delivering it he stood a moment peering towards the galleons close to the shore. They would have to turn out by yonder headland and there might be overtaken. Just at the point of the headland, he calculated, they might be overtaken. At the point—but what was happening to the point? It seemed to be moving, protracting itself. No; it was a ship, its blunt nose peering round the corner. It slid all into view. A galley. Another followed. Three: four: five. A tense silence fell upon the *Retribution*. It was not only that the men held their peace. The wind too had ceased. They had been led into a trap.

No more exuberance, no more savage exultation on board the *Retribution*. Tight-lipped the men returned to their places, realizing that this was no holiday adventure now, but a fight to the finish. As Dick went below he saw the five galleys, in crescent formation, their oars dipping and flashing, crawling towards the English ship like beetles over the clean blue floor of the sea.

The issue was wellnigh inevitable. The English ships were scattered and heavily outnumbered. That in itself might have been by no means fatal. But their ally, the wind, had deserted and they had practically no steerage-way. Save when the *Retribution* yawed round with the tide, she could not bring her heavy guns to bear on the galleys that manœuvred to be always dead in front of her. The galleons poured in volleys from long range, while the armament of the galleys, mounted upon their fore-castles and firing over the bows, could rake her from stem to stern almost without reply.

Of the fight that followed Dick had no continuity of remembrance, only a jumble of impressions—photo-graphed for ever on his brain. A volley from the demi-cannon battery laid by Martin as the ship swung round, that smashed to matchwood the port oar-bank of one of the galleys, so that she lay on the sea helpless like a bird trailing broken wing. A grinding jar as the foremost galleon lay aboard them, and the appalling outcry of shrieks and groans when Martin fired a point-blank broad-side of chain-shot into her rowers' benches. Rushing up into the waist to aid the fighting-men, who in morion and corselet were struggling against a toppling wave of boarders. The savage bearded face of a Spaniard that sud-denly went blank and silly as Dick thrust him through the heart.

Then a bump, flinging half the fighters on their faces. A galley had come up on the port beam. Men high on her mast flinging grapnels into the *Retribution's* rigging. A familiar figure, Rudgeley, his fears all foundered, cleav-ing through the press, running up the rigging, hacking with his dagger at the grapnel ropes, severing them; then his body jerking convulsively and dropping mortally wounded on the deck.

The first rush of invaders rolled back. Stink-pots dropped into the waist and the Englishmen staggering about, half suffocated. A fresh wave, a great ninth wave of Spaniards tumbling on to the deck. Martin's red beard rampant, a fiery signal appearing in a dozen places at once, it seemed, leaving destruction in its wake. The automatic cut, thrust and parry of his own arm. Blood strangely spurting from it, though he had felt no pain. A sword whistling over his head as he slipped on the bloody deck.

The final scramble of the defenders on to the poop and forecastle, whence breech-loading guns had been dealing out havoc impartially amongst the combatants in the waist. The last desperate stand with Trevaskis, Martin and a dozen others on the poop. The giant blows of Martin, the rock-like, obstinate resistance of Trevaskis. Then his hand raised in surrender—to spare the inevitable slaughter of his surviving men. The lull, the sudden cessation of sound that cut like a sword sheer through the hellish din. And all too late, as if in mockery, a cool breath of wind on his cheek; the sails of the *Ark* bellying far astern, carrying her out of the jaws of destruction. The *Mary of Lyme* lay inert alongside a galley. The fourth, which had helped to storm her, had afterwards come across to settle the issue on the *Retribution*.

But the battle was not quite over yet. The remaining Englishmen were put aboard a galley, which then drew away from her. Roger Trevaskis was kept on board with the Spanish captain and his prize-crew. A scuffle and a shout on the deck. All eyes on the galleys turned back to the English ship. Trevaskis had broken from his captors and rushed below. A few instants after there came a heaven-shattering explosion. The *Retribution* seemed to erupt with flame, like a volcano. Spars, planks, bodies were flung at the remote sky: and in a few moments nothing remained of the *Retribution* and her Spanish captors but a wreckage smoking on the sea's face. Trevaskis had fired the magazine, fired his last shot.

CHAPTER XVIII

Now followed a period of such sustained agony that all Dick's previous sufferings seemed to him but pin-pricks of discomfort. Furious at the last catastrophe, the loss of the *Retribution* and their comrades on board her, the Spaniards were in no mood to exercise clemency towards the prisoners. Some were sent to Spain, where the Inquisitors doubtless wrought their will upon them; some to slave in the mines of Panama; Dick, Martin and two score more were chained on the galleys to replace the oarsmen who had been disabled in the battle.

Five abreast they sat, straining at the unwieldy oars, nothing between their bowed heads and the savage heat of the sun, while up and down the raised platform that bisected the length of the vessel moved incessantly a Spanish under-officer, slashing at the weary oarsmen with whip or prodding them with a long goad. Salt spray and dirt rotted their clothing to rags; brackish water and cindery meat reduced them almost to skeletons; their skins were burnt black by the sun, the prey of vermin, chafed by the friction of oars. Nearly half of them died, their bodies exhausted by fever and wounds, their hearts broken by the relentless routine: these were thrown overboard like carrion as soon as they fainted at the oars. Dick himself missed such a fate by a hair's breadth: for the wound in his arm so tormented him that every pull at the oar was a fresh stab. But somewhere in him he had his father's greatest legacy, a kind of steely endurance that suffering could bend but never break; a white-hot flame of life, not to be extinguished by many waters.

So, after long days during which he moved, backward

136

forward, backward forward, in a sort of animal stupor that took no account of time or place, tortured to breaking-point by every clockwork movement, sun and spray healed his wound and life flooded slowly back.

Those of the captive Englishmen who survived this ordeal were toughened by it so that their bodies became like steel and whipcord : nothing now could weary muscle or daunt heart. They scarcely felt the flick of the Spanish lashes. Fires of anger smouldered sullenly in their eyes which boded ill for the Spanish officers who smiled indifferently at the straining backs of their enemies; to speak aloud was to invite the unerring whip; but ways and means were soon devised, slight signs and gestures, messages passed through unmoving mouths : and at any time after the first few weeks, had opportunity offered, they could have sprung into concerted action as one man.

It was this opportunity they awaited, tense and desperate, as the outlaw tiger awaits the false move of its victims. The galley was coasting south towards the Isthmus, convoying the treasure-laden galleons which had lured Trevaskis to his defeat. When they had arrived at their destination, the galleons joined company with a large treasure fleet bound for Spain, while the galleys were beached so that the battle's damage might be made good before they resumed their patrol. The galley-slaves were taken ashore, chained hand and foot, under an armed guard. Every man of them knew that now, if ever, was his chance of liberty. The Spaniards knew it, too, and their vigilance did not sleep.

The galley on which Dick and Martin laboured was more severely battered than the rest; and the task of repair taking longer, she was left behind to complete it and overtake the others as soon as might be. Every morning our hero's gang was marched into the forest beyond the

THE BRAVERY OF MARTIN.

town to hew wood. It was weary work, for they had the weight of chains to bear as well as the weight of axes. Slowly the slouched figures moved at their tasks; but every man's eye was watchful as a kestrel's under his lowering lids. Dick and Martin covertly regarded the soldiers who stood around them with sword and pistol ready.

Then one morning there was a whirring in the air and flickers of sudden light. Something with feathers appeared in the throat of the nearest guard. He made a queer bubbling noise and slipped to the ground. Groans, shouts, thudding sounds all about them, as soldiers and prisoners alike fell victim to the invisible death. For a second the survivors stood dumbfounded. Then the whole party sprang into life. But the prisoners moved a split second before the soldiers, fell upon them, smashing and strangling with the heavy chains. Clusters of men demoniacally struggling: then the cluster would dissolve, leaving a body motionless upon the ground.

Martin now took command, bidding the rest not to stir a foot.

"Lads," he said, "we are in deadlier peril this moment than ever from the Spaniard. These be Indian arrows. The Indians are all about us, and they make no distinction betwixt Spanish and English: the white man is their enemy. There is but one hope. If ye have any regard for your lives or mine own, do not attempt to follow me."

And then he did the bravest thing Dick ever saw. Holding out his chained arms he walked slowly and calmly towards the belt of trees where the Indians were lurking. Dick covered his face. He could not bear to look. It seemed so certain that, at the next step, the poisoned death would fly at Martin out of the gloom. He heard a rattling of fetters and Martin's voice, speaking in the

careless jovial tones of one inviting boon-companions to
share a gallon of beer.

"Avast there, my hearties, my bully black-skins! We
are friends, we are friends, so come out and let's see your
dusky snouts!"

There was a stone-dead silence, while Martin's life
trembled in the balance. Then the wood began to move;
dark-eyed, flat-nosed, with brightly painted bodies, moving like wild animals on their supple shining limbs, the
Indians cautiously emerged. Martin had won. Whether
it was his audacious courage; or that the blood-lust had
now cooled in them; or whether Martin's wild and majestic appearance struck god-like upon their simple hearts,
none can tell. But they crowded round Martin, jabbering
like monkeys, admiring his stature, timidly prodding his
iron muscles. One, with great daring, reached up and
tugged his beard, whereupon the rest broke into cries of
childish glee. Martin encircled the waists of the two
nearest with manacled hands and vented a cannonade of
laughter which caused the nearest to shy away like
startled deer: then rattled his fetters, pointed to his comrades and his mouth.

The Indians signed to them to follow. Seeing a certain
hesitation amongst them, Martin cried:

"Yarely, boys! Fear not. Ye are too stringy meat to
find yourselves yet in a cannibal's cook-pot!"

The Indians led them some miles down obscure tracks
into the interior: a slow, wearisome march, for the chains
hampered them sorely. Arrived at the village, they had
their fetters knocked off and sat down on skins in the
chief's hut, and gorged themselves on venison, bread,
potatoes, fruit and fish, the first square meal they had
eaten since leaving England. Ere they retired to sleep that
night, Martin called his men about him and spoke:

" Lads, we are not out of the wood yet. We are but a handful in a hostile country. The Dons will be on our heels as soon as they find our party return not. And I know not how long we may trust these Indians. Mark me, I have had some commerce with the savage. Ye see them now, merry and mischievous as children. But they are touchy and treacherous too : they are like animals, that bite on suspicion, without warning. One blow given, one harsh word—and they'll slice your scalps off as readily as to-day they feed ye. If I see any one of ye give offence, I strangle that man with my own hands. But show no fear neither. Ye know how a dog will spring at a man whom he feels to be afraid of him. 'Tis the same with these gentry. And keep your eyes skinned for means of escape. I trow ye wish not to linger out your days in these out-landish regions."

The council broke up. Dick lay down to rest with a new feeling of admiration for Martin. His shrewd cool-headed-ness; his instinctive knowledge of the dark workings of savage minds. He felt thoroughly ashamed of having sometimes looked down on his friend for his rough ways, his superstition, his ignorance of book-learning. How un-important such defects seemed when balanced against the man's natural wisdom and leadership.

Early the next morning the Indians led them to a broad river near by, in which every savage—man, woman and child—plunged and frolicked. They showed amaze-ment that the Englishmen were slow to follow : but white men at this time felt little disgust at unclean-liness and did not often find themselves in water unless they had fallen into it. Dick tugged at Martin's arm.

" Prithee, look at yon Indian !"

" Aye. He is floating across the river on an horse's

skin. They sew them up and blow them out. 'Tis common
practice amongst these savages."

" Marry," exclaimed Dick, joking, " we must e'en pro-
vide ourselves with the like and float to England on
them !"

A sudden spark kindled in Martin's eye.

" Float to England on them. Beshrew me if thy random
fancy hath not hit near the bull !" he muttered, medi-
tatively fingering his beard.

Dick was mystified by the extraordinary effect of his
idle words: still mystified when, after their return to the
village, he noticed Martin deep in sign-talk with the
Indian chief, a huge pipe of tobacco passing between them.
The mystery was cleared up that afternoon. Martin called
the Englishmen about him, and amid flashing of teeth
and hoarse oaths of approval proposed certain plans and
gave each man certain directions.

As night was falling a line of men stole out from the
village in the direction of the sea. At the head went
Indian guides. After them the Englishmen: their faces,
legs, and arms were blackened with charcoal; some carried
weapons, others more curious objects. Stealthily as pan-
thers they crept on to the shore. Palm trees murmured to
each other. To their right, moored in the roadstead, the
black bulk of the galley loomed sinister through the night.
The guides merged again into the darkness behind them.
Sentries on the quays marched to and fro under the moon-
less sky. A few words were muttered at the sea's edge,
drowned by the sleepy plash of the surf.

Drowned, too, was the sound of the Englishmen taking
to the water on their inflated skins and paddling with feet
and hands towards the galley. Martin and Dick, on a
great ox-skin, were twenty yards in front of the rest,
Martin paddling, Dick holding oakum and brimstone out

FIRING THE GALLEY.

of reach of the splashing wavelets. Laughter and talk could be heard from the galley's occupants, unconscious of the approach of this weird armada.

Dick saw the stern-post looming up before him. Martin gripped it. Dick, standing up precariously on the skin, stuffed his materials into the space between rudder and stern; lit tinder; kindled the stuff. Smoke trickled, poured up; then flame. Martin and Dick hastily edged round along the galley's side as the guards, roused by the smell of burning, tumbled pell-mell towards the stern. A dozen skins clustered like giant bubbles around the vessel's prow. The Englishmen clambered noiselessly on to the deck. The Spanish guards, busy extinguishing the flames, heard a pitter-patter behind them. Their shrieks of horror as they turned and saw devilish black faces grinning at them were stifled in their throats by the grip of two-score steely hands. And ere the townspeople, alarmed by the spurts of flame from the galley, had launched their boats, the Englishmen were rowing steadily out to sea, leaving nothing behind but the monstrous skin bubbles and some Spanish corpses floating in the water as a clue to the galley's disappearance.

Two days later the lookouts on the *Ark*, which had been following their captive comrades at a wary distance in the remote hope of rescue, sighted the lateen sails of a galley standing eastward towards them. At six hundred yards the *Ark's* gunner plopped a ball across the galley's bows and was electrified to see the tiny figures on her deck leaping—gesticulating in what was apparently the last stage of lunacy; a figure detached itself from the mass, tore off its white shirt, and ran frantically up the rigging, waving it. As the *Ark* drew nearer, its amazed crew saw that this figure wagged a huge red beard. It was Martin! Their comrades were saved!

PART FOUR
PRIVY CONSPIRACY

CHAPTER XIX

EARLY in the spring of 1566, two years after Dick had set forth upon his ocean travels, Cynthia was riding through the woods southward of Clifford Castle. She had ridden this way times out of mind since that fateful evening when Dick had walked out of her life into the deepening shadows. No word of his fortunes had found its way back. His name was never mentioned at the castle save as one mentions the dead: and Cynthia herself, though she never quite lost hope of his return, came more and more to think of it as a miracle—an event that only boundless faith could bring to pass. So, as she rode, she said to herself over and over, "He is going to come back, he is going to come back," while the breeze in the pines echoed the sighing of her heart.

This was a morning for miracles, too. New life was stirring and stretching under the ferny earth, under the bark of trees. Miraculously blue, after the leaden hues of winter, showed the sky through laced branches. Cynthia felt the spring in her blood, too; not the riotous surge that in childhood had set her laughter wildly trilling and prompted her to madcap feats, but a fuller, steadier flow. She was a woman grown now. Dick could scarcely have recognized the young stately figure that moved amongst the trees: the last two years had strengthened the contours of lip and brow, sealed her face with a finer beauty. What did Dick look like now? she wondered. Would she know him when he came back, a man? If he came back. No, *when* he came. She must never begin to doubt. But would that he were here now, not seas away: for things were happening at the castle which, she suspected, needed a man's strength and resolution.

Even as she revolved these things in her mind there was a crackling near by, and two men stepped out of the trees. Bearded, ragged, wild-seeming they were. Cynthia gripped her riding-whip and went a little pale: but she stood her ground as the men advanced. Then something familiar about the slighter figure—the lilting walk, or perhaps the hair whose gold had not been quite bleached away by torrid suns—made her senses dizzy as a whirl-pool. A voice said, "Cynthia!"—a gruff, manly voice she scarcely recognized—and strong arms caught her as she slipped from her horse. Dick was come home.

It was like that afternoon on the tower, Dick thought, as he held her close. The seas that had lain between them were rolled away like a scroll by this moment. It seemed they had never been parted. Her eyes opened; she put up a hand and touched his hair, as if to make sure he was real. Then they kissed and called each other's names, the fond, faithful creatures, while Martin emitted two por-tentous coughs and fell a-studying of a newly formed chestnut bud with the severe intentness of a chemist staring into a crucible.

Presently Dick called him, and he came up to the pair beaming like the noonday and made a profound obeisance to Cynthia; whereupon she staggered the good mariner by flinging her arms round his neck and impetuously kissing him.

"So thou art Martin," she cried. "Dick used often to speak of thee. And now thou hast brought him back safe to me. Aye, safe. And 'tis thou didst save him, dear Martin, I warrant. Quick, tell me of it; tell me!"

"Why, as to that, 'twas little saving he needed. Thou shouldst have seen him pricking that Spaniard through the midriff—— A curse on my graceless tongue! These be no tales for a gentle woman's ears."

" Nay, Martin, I'll not be denied. My ears are none such brittle stuff that tales of valour shall shiver them."

And she drew Martin down on the turf beside her and Dick and pulled his beard till she had dragged every incident of their adventures out of him. The voyage; the mutiny; the attack; the galley; the escape; how the *Ark* had cruised another year, greatly daring, in hostile waters, and returned with a bellyful of treasure; and how Dick would not linger so much as an hour at Southampton, but must needs press on toward Clifford, ragged as he was, to find his Cynthia, outdistancing the servant that rode behind with their belongings. As he unfolded their tale Dick interrupted frequently to paint in brighter colour the part Martin had played; for, from his own account, one would suppose that he had been merely a mild spectator : while Cynthia's breath came fast and her eyes glowed like Desdemona's listening to the exploits of Othello.

" And now," she said, when the sailor's narrative was finished and he was rewarding his dry throat with the contents of a leather bottle, " what designest thou to do, Dick? Thou canst not enter the castle, or Sir Giles——"

Martin spluttered out a mouthful of ale, bellowing : " Sir Giles? Ha! Yon viper had escaped my memory. I will instantly repair to the castle and squeeze his poisonous life out of his skinny throat!"

" Whisht, Martin," the girl exclaimed; " 'tis ill shouting in these woods. Even the trees at Clifford have grown ears. And methinks thy sinew shall little avail against stone walls and a score armed men."

" Armed men?" said Dick. " Why, surely thy uncle keepeth warlike preparation against the return of a dispossessed orphan—and one that should be a ghost, for all he knoweth."

" 'Tis not on thy account, Dick. He believeth thee dead,

to my best knowledge—though sometimes I am not sure. He is deep as the Pit and subtler than the Serpent. Thou mayst not fathom his thoughts. But I misdoubt me he flieth at higher game. I have heard——"

She broke off, peering fixedly into the recesses of the wood; in graver tones resumed:

"There have been strange doings of late at Clifford. Comings and goings by night; secret conference; Stephen Sant is vigilant again in the passages, and one standeth often sentry upon the tower top. That priest—thou rememberest him, Dick—haunteth the castle; I suspect he may be a Jesuit, an emissary from Spain. But yesterevening I ventured through the secret passage—some instinct led me—and heard the priest and my uncle talking. 'The true faith shall be established then and the infidel Queen discomfited,' one said. And another: 'To-morrow night our friends assemble here; that shall be the birthday of our fortunes.' I could hear no more. But mischief was in their voices. And this morning I ran into a servingman and felt the shape of a poniard beneath his clothing."

"'To-morrow night,' said he," muttered Dick. "That is to-night. Martin, it were well for us to attend this conclave of 'the true faith.' What sayest thou?"

"Nay, Dick; have a care!" cried Cynthia. "These men are dangerous as hunted rats. They would dispatch thee without scruple if thou settedst foot in their secrecy."

"Then must secrecy be countered by secrecy. This is my plan: Thou must return to the castle instantly, Cynthia, lest thy tarrying should awake suspicion. Martin and I will watch from the forest's edge till nightfall. When it seemeth that all the conspirators—if so they be— are safe within walls, we will sally through the secret passage and attempt to overhear their conference. Should we discover aught of vital import to the State, we will ride post-haste to London and lay our evidence before the Secretary."

" 'Tis well," Cynthia replied; "but one thing: it may hap that ye will need means of entrance to the castle when ye return. I cannot think the underground way will ever be left unguarded. There is one of the servants who is faithful to me. Hoot thrice like an owl under the postern betwixt the hours of eight and eleven at night, and he or I will be on the watch and make shift to open for thee. The next time we meet thou shalt not be rid of me so easily, Dick."

With these words and a long look at Dick, the girl rode off. The two friends then awaited the arrival of Dick's servant, one of the sailors from the *Retribution*; and when he had joined them they mounted their horses, which were picketed near by, and all three made their way slowly through the forest till they could see the castle's bulk showing huge and dismal through the thickly growing trees. Here, in a dense patch of holly, they halted and hid themselves while the shadow of the walls lengthened over the intervening ground. Four men they saw, as they watched, riding up at intervals of half an hour or so and tapping upon the postern. Each time it was opened almost as soon as knuckles struck wood, and with a furtive look behind the man would step quickly through. The secret passage, it seemed, was only used for emergency. The evening was strangely quiet, earth and sky holding their peace, like armies on the verge of action. The sounds of the tapping on the postern were carried faintly to the hidden listeners, like a woodpecker's heard from far— two short raps, a pause, then three more.

Now it was quite dark. The three skulked cautiously towards the ruined cottage. A stick cracked under Martin's foot. They stopped dead: so loud the noise seemed it must surely have penetrated those massy walls. They moved on. The ruin gleamed palely in front of them.

"Andrew," Dick whispered to the servant, "thou must stay here. This is our one avenue of retreat. Guard it as thou wouldst guard our lives."

He touched the spring and the section of wall whirred rustily back. Dick plunged through, Martin following him. Darkness was solid: one had to push against it as against a horribly yielding jelly of flesh. They whispered to each other, their faces not a foot apart, yet could see no vestige of the lips that whispered back. Now a different carriage of their bodies told them they were moving upward; and through the shuffle of their steps and the dripping of water they heard a hum of voices, which grew louder as they neared the door.

CHAPTER XX

THREE of these voices Dick could recognize. Sir Giles' softly lisping, yet with the menace of the panther's foot padding softly through jungle; the calm tones of the priest, calm and cool and detached as a voice speaking unseen in some high-pillared cathedral; and an occasional harsh jangle when Stephen Sant interjected some remark. Sir Giles spoke, so quietly that Dick's straining ears could not catch half he said.

"The six are ready. . . . Methinks the blow shall not fall this time upon air. . . . 'Tis your task to release the Queen of Scots and show her to the people. . . . Philip's armada will be on the seas. While the kingdom yet reeleth he will strike home: all the faithful oppressed will rise then against the usurper."

Then he proceeded to the details of the plot. The names of Babington and Ballard recurred frequently, names unknown to Dick. While a part of his mind stored up every crumb and item of conspiracy, another part began to be strangely fascinated by the speaker's level, flowing tones: he felt himself yielding to an unwilling admiration for Sir Giles' courage—for courage it was to attempt such an enterprise where so many had failed, a handful of men against a kingdom. He shook himself. This would never do. His cousin was damned out of his own mouth. A stranger's voice spoke:

"The train is laid now and must be fired. But I fear the issue. The fox, Walsingham, hath never been caught sleeping before. It cannot be that he is altogether in the dark as to our purpose."

"Doubtless he hath heard rumour. But what can he do? That painted harridan, Elizabeth, keepeth her watchdog on the chain. She will never allow him to act till clear proof is laid before her. And this time the proof will be his mistress's dead body. Let him act then," returned Sir Giles venomously.

Martin could not restrain himself.

" The toad-spotted traitor! Let me lay finger on——" he hissed.

" Hush, Martin, or thou wilt betray all!"

There was silence in the room. The two friends stood rigid as the walls about them, fearing that Martin's indignation had penetrated into the council. Sir Giles broke the silence.

" Gentlemen, let our conference be adjourned. From henceforth, 'tis weapons not words must be our business. The papers bearing on our plans shall find safe repository in yon chest. Come, sirs."

There was a crackling of parchment, a receding confusion of footsteps. Dick's heart hammered madly.

" Martin," he whispered, " if we can but come by those papers, our case shall be doubly proven."

He pushed delicately at the door. Through the chink could be seen a section of room, dark but for the firelight. A little wider. No one was there. They stepped in: moved wraith-like towards the chest. Dick opened it, and bent over to scrutinize the documents piled therein. A resinous stick on the fire was hissing faintly. While his eyes rapidly ran over the titles of these documents his ears were registering independently the noise from the fire. And slowly, as the trickle through a leak warns the sailor of danger, so did premonition of disaster trickle into Dick's mind with that queer hissing. He found himself listening to it consciously. Strange: it was not continuous, as such a noise should be, but came at regular intervals, like breathing.

He straightened up, listening. His heart gave a shock-ing bump and stood still. There was a shadow on the wall where no shadow had been a few seconds before. And it was like the silhouette of a demon upon the walls of hell, nightmare tall, hideously snouted. Dick sprang round, Martin at his side. They were confronted by Stephen Sant, who had stepped silently from behind the arras at their backs. All this happened in a few seconds, and it took another fraction of a second for Dick to realize that they were trapped: Martin's voice must have been heard, and the room left empty but for Sant, baited with those papers to entice them in.

Luckily for them, Stephen too was momentarily para-lyzed on seeing the countenance of the slighter figure that turned upon him. His pallid face seemed to fall in, like dead ash, and the spark in his eyes was extinguished with terror beholding at arm's length one who must have risen from the dead. His mouth opened in a sobbing whimper. A little noise, but enough to warn those who watched outside the door: they burst in to see Stephen Sant, hurled backward by Martin, flying through the air with arms and legs whirling like vanes of a crazy windmill, while Martin and Dick were leaping towards the secret door. It slammed in the pursuers' faces, giving the fugitives a ten-yard start through the tunnel. That was not enough. As they ran, doubled ape-like, down the slope, Martin panted to Dick:

"'Tis useless. . . . They will catch us in the open. . . . I will stem their advance. . . . Do thou escape, and God be with thee."

He halted. Dick squeezed his arm in the darkness, then hurried on. He heard the crash, the startled oaths, as the first of the pursuers charged into Martin. Then the sounds grew fainter and he could but guess at the progress of that subterranean battle. The tunnel was too narrow to allow one man to squeeze past another, so Martin had to deal with only one at a time. Furiously his fists flailed at the blank darkness in front of him, now thudding into flesh, now cracking against stone. In and out, in and out, tireless as pistons, his arms worked, battering two of his assailants into oblivion and choking the passage with their bodies. He might have held them at bay indefinitely, even made good his own escape, had not a man, lunging forward with a sword over his comrades' bodies, skewered Martin through the shoulder and disabled him. Dourly still he fought, but his strength was ebbing through the wound, and soon he was borne to the ground, and the servitors trampled over him and passed on.

But his stand had given Dick a longer lease of escape. He was now at the far end of the passage and dragging Andrew, who was reluctant to leave Martin, towards the woods. Even as they emerged from the ruin the postern grated open and figures streamed out to intercept them. As the pursuit crashed into the copse, they leapt to horse, slashing the third animal across the quarters so that it plunged away into the gloom ahead, and galloped blindly off through the whipping boughs while a random volley of oaths and arrows crackled about their ears.

When they came out on the track, Dick yelled to Andrew:

"Spare not the spur! We ride for the Queen's life as well as our own."

Like wild-fire they tore along the springy ground, turf fountaining up behind them. After ten minutes Dick made sign to halt. They listened intently. No surge of pursuit sounded through the forest. Exultation shook their hearts; but it turned in a moment to cold dismay as a distant sound floated towards them, a clear tolling like the tolling of a passing-bell, the bay of mastiffs upon a trail.

"If we can but gain the highroad, master," exclaimed Andrew, "surely they would dare pursue no further."

Dick had his doubts about this. Where so much was at stake, Sir Giles was not likely to relinquish his prey for fear of chance eyes witnessing the kill. However, he plied whip and spur and they fled onward, the trees flicking past, the solemn belling of the hounds striking ever clearer through the drumming hooves. And now the crowning mischance of that unlucky night fell upon them. Andrew's horse stepped in a rabbit hole, turned a somersault and lay floundering on the turf, a leg broken. The sailor was shot yards over its head and winded in the fall. When he had breath to speak, he said:

"Ride on, Master Dick. Linger not for me. The dice are cogged against me. Thy horse will not bear us both, and a worthier life than mine is in jeopardy."

Dick was frantic, torn between his mission and his affection for the faithful sailor. He made up his mind.

"Nay, Andrew, Queen or no Queen, I'll not leave thee to these ravening brutes."

Andrew picked up his cudgel and limped towards Dick, saying:

"I reck little of the life of any sovereign. 'Tis of thine I spoke."

And raising the cudgel he thwacked it mightily on Dick's horse, so that it sprang away and carried him a hundred yards before he could pull it up. Turning in the saddle, he could see no trace of Andrew. That heroic, simple man had darted into the trees so that there might be less chance of Dick's returning to rescue him. Now Dick remembered how he carried the safety of the realm on his head, so he turned away, sick at heart, yet determined that Andrew's sacrifice should not have been in vain.

How great this sacrifice was he did not come to realize till many days were past. Fearing that the dogs might follow Dick's trail, not his own, the sailor waited in the shadow of the trees till they appeared, three of them, running like a resistless tide, at the far end of the glade. Then he stepped into the open, bracing himself squarely as so often he had done against the shock of tempest. The first mastiff's skull was shattered by his cudgel; the second rolled over howling, maimed by a vicious kick; the third sprang home and snapped its teeth in the sailor's neck. But Andrew's fingers and Andrew's spirit were as indomitable as the hound; and the riders who galloped up a few moments later found man and mastiff locked in death, the man's throat torn half away, his hands an iron collar about the dog's strangled neck.

Such was Andrew's end, like that of many heroes, unseen and unsung.

"Waste no time on this carrion," snarled Sir Giles; "the hounds have played their part. 'Tis evident the pretty young spy, my cousin, headeth for London. He must be headed off."

The cavalcade thundered on. Dick's horse, which had a day's journey already to its credit, began to weary: and pausing for a moment to breathe him, Dick heard the muffled drum-roll of pursuing hooves behind him. Fatal to continue on his known course. He swerved aside into the trees, and before his horse had trampled a hundred yards through the tangle he broke out into a clearing and saw the hulk of a house in front. One lighted window leered at him. He was about to ride on when something in the hovel's shape plucked a chord of his memory.

Surely he had seen that lop-sided outline before? Yes, it was the witch's cottage.

He stood undecided. Should he ride forward, banking on the chance that his enemies would not turn off on his trail, or seek the dubious sanctuary of the hovel and its ill-favoured occupant? Even as he debated, he heard the pursuit coming roaring like a hurricane through the wood. There was a sinister lull; then he heard shouts, saw torches darting amid the trees. They must have had a sharp-eyed tracker with them who had discerned the breaking-off of hoof-prints along the ride or the wreckage of branches where Dick had burst into the wood's tangle. Dick had a hundred yards' grace. He rode swiftly along the edge of the clearing round to the far side of the house, then dismounted under its cover. He must be rid of the steed that had served him so well. No time to picket it deeper in the forest. He slashed it without mercy, sending it galloping madly into the further reaches of the night, skulked up to the ramshackle door, and strode in.

The old woman was there, crouched before the fire. She started up at Dick's entry, backing away from him with trembling hands raised to ward him off. Then, as he came within the firelight's radius, she halted, stared earnestly at him, and quavered out:

"God's mercy! Why, 'tis my golden-haired gallant! Prithee, young master, what make ye here at this dead hour?"

An approaching clamour of voices supplied the answer.

"Hide me, good dame, hide me! I stand in deadliest peril," Dick cried.

The woman gazed wildly round. In that bare, one-roomed hovel there seemed covert for nothing bigger than a flea. Advancing torches began to show ruddy through the open top of the half-door. The witch hobbled to her bed; flung off the blanket; pushed Dick deep into the yielding mass of branch and fern; and hastily smoothed fern and blanket over him. Wriggling further into the evil-smelling softness, Dick heard an imperious rapping on the door. Then Sir Giles' voice:

"Is there anyone within?"

A mumble from the witch. Footsteps tramping. A sharp intake of breath as the intruders beheld the hag's hideous features. Sir Giles speaking again:

"Hast heard a rider pass this way? We pursue a murderer, a notorious outlaw."

"No, your honour, no; indeed I heard naught: but I am an old woman and sorely stricken with the deafness."

"Marry, but thou heardest me well enough and I not speaking over-loud. Friends, I like this not. Search the place. And thou, noisome beldam, play me not false, or I will——"

Sir Giles' hissing threats were lost in the whimpers and chattering of teeth as he shook the old woman viciously to and fro. Another voice spoke.

"Have a care, my lord, this woman is a known witch and may take fell revenge. There is no one here. We have pried into every mouse-hole and crevice."

"A plague on your old-wives' fancies! I care not a straw for witch or warlock. What, ye laggards, have ye not even searched yon bed? Cannot a body lie in it as easily as on it? We shall soon see."

Petrified, Dick heard a swish: the sound of sword drawn from scabbard. The blade was raised aloft in Sir Giles' hand, about to stab downward through blanket and fern, when a new voice shouted excitedly from the door:

"Away, my masters! To horse! We have found his hoof-prints on the far side of the clearing."

There was a ragged outcry of voices; a scramble for the door; then the clink of stirrups and a dying thunder of hooves. Dick struggled out of his retreat and for the second time kissed the brave old woman, who had indeed turned into a guardian goddess at his hour of need.

CHAPTER XXI

EARLY next morning, while dank mist still scarfed the trees, Dick arose and pondered his plans. Whether Sir Giles found the riderless steed or no, he was bound to realize soon that the fugitive had tricked him. What would happen then? Every available man would be used to block the roads. There was no safety for him till he was lodged in Sir Francis Walsingham's house. Time was running short. Though the attempt on the Queen's life was not due for a sennight, there was Martin to consider. It was unbelievable that he too could have escaped. He might, indeed, be dead already. But it was more probable that, if he had not been killed in the tunnel, Sir Giles would keep him as a kind of hostage, would put him to the question. And knowing what would be the manner of that question, Dick shuddered in his soul.

No, he must move apace. To travel on by-roads was to delay and increase Martin's danger—he could not think of his friend as dead. Moreover, the enemy might believe him more likely to keep away from the highroad, and therefore leave it less well guarded. But to adventure on the highroad in his present guise would be madness. Doubtless description of him would be circulated amongst the watchers, and once recognized he could expect no mercy from assassin's dagger though he stood in crowded market-place or jovial tap-room.

The old woman now broke in on his meditation with bread and a draught of that bitter, strangely invigorating herb-brew which he had received from her hands two years before. He placed his situation briefly before her. She mumbled.

"Disguise, sayest thou? Shall old Betsy make a girl of thee?"

And hobbling over to a corner, she picked up a villain-
ously blunt knife. Dick was in considerable apprehension
lest her wits had veered round to murder. However, it was
his young beard, not his life, she aimed to shear away. And
Dick stood groaning while the ancient blade tore away
at his stubble. Then the woman laid a heap of ragged
clothes in his arms, a skirt and a cloak; and Dick, doffing
some of his own, put on the foul-smelling raiment. So
disguised, with his tanned face and springy gait, he looked
the picture of some vagrant gipsy girl. He paused but to
feel, safe slung from his neck, the ring on which so many
fortunes depended, and to bid the old woman a grateful
adieu: then he walked out towards the wood, crossing
the frontier into territory that seemed all his enemy's.
There he cut himself a stout staff of ash, and after an
hour's walking came out on the highway to London. He
had nothing but a ring, a staff, a little money, and his own
wits to take him there.

Though he had no illusions about the difficulties that
lay before him, his heart could not help being infected by
the blitheness of that spring morning, and soon he was
striding along, whistling as carelessly as the blackbirds
and thrushes in the wayside copses. Everything seemed so
innocent. Could murder lurk under that blue sky, among
the bland green of meadow and pasture that sunned themselves in the spring's warmth? Treading mile after mile
unmolested, exchanging cheerful greetings with his fellow-
wayfarers or being totally ignored by some passing grandee
—nobleman, bailiff or merchant—Dick's vigilance was
lulled. He could almost believe that yesterday night had
been a bad dream, that no pitfalls lay ahead.

His sense of security was shattered, however, when he
entered the environs of Winchester. Two men were idling
against the wall of an inn: they appeared to be absorbed

in a game of knucklebones; but as Dick approached he noticed one of them peer at him, straighten up, and tread —seemingly by accident—on his companion's toe. Dick's first instinct was to cut and run for it; but realizing how infallibly that must betray him, he clutched his cloak closer about him and made to walk straight past the men. He was not to get away so easily as that, though. One of them stepped across his path and accosted him.

"Whither away, my comely Egyptian? Shouldst not be travelling unattended, a buxom girl like thee."

Dick was relieved to see no glint of suspicion in the man's eye. His disguise must be good. He tuned his voice to a woman's higher pitch and replied:

"I go to Surrey, an't please you, to join my tribe."

"Hast seen aught of a young man, on horseback or foot, a golden-haired young man? He is a friend of ours, and we expect him hourly, having certain pressing business with him," he added, chuckling unpleasantly.

"Nay, sir, I call to mind none such. I prithee let me pass."

"Not so fast, not so fast, my dusky doxy," said the man, laying an unsavoury hand upon Dick's arm; "the day hath not passed noon. Thou shalt drain a dram with us to help thee on thy way."

Here Dick, in his impatience, mislaid prudence and attempted to drag his arm away. In so doing the hood of the cloak was drawn back and his close-cropped hair disclosed. The man was so taken aback by this revelation that he involuntarily loosened his grip. Dick sprang away, and holding up his skirt darted down the street towards the centre of the town, the two knaves in hot pursuit. Cumbered as he was, he could not run his fastest: the men gained on him; he expected every moment to feel a dagger between his shoulder-blades; but when the toe of the bigger man was almost rasping on his heel,

Dick collided round a corner with three individuals. He hurriedly slipped his hood back into position while the individuals were recovering their composure, and his recent pursuers turned aside to feign acute interest in the goods of an adjacent stall.

Dick now found himself the target of a battery of six eyes. He saw by their badges that he had providentially run into a posse of constables. The senior of these stepped forward, a man whose noble paunch consorted well with the dignity of his office; his eyes were small and stupid as a pig's, their complacent stare promising no great danger for any quick-witted evil-doer he might attempt to lay by the heels.

"So-ho, wench," this worthy wheezed; "assault the majesty of the law? That constitutes a felony, and is punishable with stocks or pillory. How say ye, my bullies; cometh this not under the meaning of the act?"

His fellow-headboroughs, a fish-faced, undersized old man and a huge moon-calf of a fellow with legs like Norman pillars, murmured assent—clearly impressed by the legal gibberish of their sergeant.

Dick mastered a strong inclination to poke the speaker in his excessive belly, and whined out:

"Oh, sirs, punish me not! I am but a poor gipsy wench, travelling to join her tribe. I meant no indignity to the law, but was fleeing from yon two scoundrels who sought to detain me."

He turned to point where the two scoundrels stood; but they had made themselves scarce while the majesty of the law was regaining its breath. The sergeant, whose wits had been revolving as slowly and almost as audibly as rusty clockwork during Dick's speech, now resumed the attack in pompous tones.

"A gipsy, sesta? Ergo, I deprehend, a vagrant. And,

whereas all vagrants be necessitous by the law of the realm to carry license and badge, and whereas thou carriest not the badge above mentioned, ergo thou art unbadged; wherefore must the law bid thee show thy license, or—more combustibly speaking thy—er—to wit, in fact—er—thy license," he concluded lamely, his legal flow temporarily run dry.

Dick's arguments fell quite flat upon the ears of the headborough, and he was led away to the place of justice, fuming inwardly to think how the safety of the realm was being imperilled by the interference of these officious minions. However, their manifest stupidity encouraged him to be vigilant for some shift by which he might make his escape. When they arrived outside the constable's house Dick saw a horse tethered by the door, a cob whose enormous girth suggested the portly headborough as its master. On enquiry he found this to be the case; so, assuming an expression of deepest mystery, he said to the horse's owner :

"Your honour, perchance I may palliate my offence against the law by doing a slight service to thee, its noble representative. My mother, a princess of her tribe, hath store of our ancient wisdom. She hath taught me a charm by which prosperity may be assured to a man. Let me but mount thy horse's back a moment and cut seven hairs from its mane with this secret incantation, and thou shalt ride to instant fortune."

The headborough hummed and hawed a little; but his piggy eyes gleamed avariciously, and a nervous giggle from his moon-calf assistant made up his mind for him.

"Beshrew me if I fear any spell or witchery under the sun. These Egyptians have strange powers, as all men know who, like me, are acquainted with the greater world. Here is a knife."

Dick mounted slowly on to the horse, and rolling his eyes muttered, " Hocus-pocus avunculi-ranunculi horum-harum-horum," slashed the tethering rope with the knife, and was clattering down the street before the gaping mouths of the constables could ejaculate a single sound. Many an honest burgher of Winchester discussed gravely with his spouse that night the spectacle which had broken the placid surface of his life—the spectacle of a strapping gipsy wench galloping full-tilt over the cobbles on the constable's fat nag, scattering bystanders, stalls and traffic like a tropic cyclone.

The rider in question had little leisure to be aware of the impression he was creating. Even as he belaboured his horse, which showed signs of resenting this unusual burst of speed, his brain was rapidly reviewing the situation. Two nests of hornets had been stirred up now—the law and the lawless, and he could make a good guess which was the more dangerous. He was a bare mile out of the town when, looking back, he saw a cloud of dust hanging over a fold of hill. Someone had lost no time. That the someone was not the constable soon became apparent; for the chase, drawing in sight, rode in grim silence, altogether too unpleasantly efficient-looking to be mistaken for the constable and his posse.

As ill-luck had it, there was not a soul in sight on the stretch of road ahead : and Dick's horse being clearly near the end of its very short tether, he had almost given himself up to despair and decided to make a last stand for his life there on the chalky highway, when his darting eye beheld a spire of smoke rising out of a lap of ground to the right hand. Any port in a storm. He bundled off the cob, which at once fell to chewing at the hedge, and scuttled across the intervening grass towards the smoke. As he mounted the rise a quarry came into view, with a rude tent pitched amid gorse bushes near its edge, and a tall, merry-eyed rogue tending a fire in front of it.

Dick had scarcely time to gasp out a plea for succour to this individual when the pursuers came streaming over the down, having dismounted in the road. Three of them there were, the two who had previously accosted him reinforced by another. Dick's new-found friend did not pause to enquire into the merits of the case, but picked up a cudgel and dashed at the oncomers, striking woundily about him. They broke before his onslaught, and while one of their number held him in play the other two made a dash at Dick, who was standing a couple of yards from the quarry's lip. The foremost of these Dick dodged adroitly; then helped on his headlong career with a swing of his staff, so that he floundered over the edge and tumbled into the quarry, shrieking horribly. Dick then went into the other and gripped his dagger-wrist. They swayed furiously for a few seconds. A pair of arms plucked Dick's assailant off him and flung him head first into a gorse bush. The merry-eyed rogue had already broken the arm of his first antagonist; and now he watched with a mild grin while his second victim extricated himself from the gorse bush, cursing hideously, and shambled away supporting his wounded comrade to the roadside.

Dick, however, had no intention of letting them get away to give an immediate alarm. Calling his rescuer to follow, he sprinted after the men, outpaced them, and seized two of the horses. The would-be assassins were so discomfited by their warm reception that they made no protest, save for strings of oaths, when Dick and his friend led away the three horses, leaving them to share the ample bulk of the constable's cob. Returning to the quarry, Dick looked over : a body sprawled like a rag doll at the bottom, the head horridly crushed. Well, that was one less between him and success. He could spare no pity. He turned to thank his rescuer. The man was busy packing up his tent and sparse belongings, unconcerned as though such mortal scuffles were a daily exercise.

" Thou strikest out full lustily for a wench," quoth he; then, looking up and taking in Dick's appearance for the first time at leisure, exclaimed :

" Rot me, if 'tis not a cock-bird! Marry, thou goest in strange gear. Ay well, Tom Tuttlesham was never one to ask questions. Thy looks like me well. Nay, thank me not —such trifling bickerings are mightily to my taste. But wilt join company with me? My last partner fell foul of the drawlatches; I need another. Canst filch a bung, I warrant."

Dick goggling in bewilderment at this incomprehensible jargon, the merry rogue roared out:

" 'Oons, but thou art a green apprentice! To filch a bung, that is to steal a purse in the language of thieves' law."

Dick disclaimed any connection with the profession, but expressed his readiness to ride in Tom's company toward London; and, reading a kind of trustworthiness in the man's eyes, told him something of his story. It was now Tom's turn to gape amazement. When the tale was done he pondered a moment; then, clasping Dick by the hand, said :

" Certes, thou standest in need of a friend. Tom Tuttlesham hath little allegiance to Queen or Parliament, and little desire to be mixed up in affairs of State. But a stout arm and a quick wit goeth ever to his heart, and he is honoured to befriend thee."

And in ten minutes the strangely assorted couple were riding rapidly along the highroad together.

CHAPTER XXII

IN the course of the two days during which Dick bore company with Tom he learnt more of life, perhaps, than in any two years of his existence. It was not so much his thieving profession that made Tom like a native of some other world than Dick's. In those days, when visionary Eldorados had come true, and the Queen and her Court set an example of avarice and feverish desire for new luxury, it was little wonder that wealth was the ideal of the nation. Englishmen revelled in riches, or the dream of riches: yet with an exuberant, childlike delight which somehow protected them, for the most part, from the evil consequences that are wont to attend the fever of getting and spending.

If robbery was crime, then was the Queen a criminal whose purse was fattened by the piratical exploits of her sea captains; and half the nobility of the land must be criminals too, for their acres had been filched from the dispossessed monks scarce a hundred years before. No, it was not Tom's profession that opened Dick's eyes to modes of life beyond his experience. It was the man's insouciance, his gay disregard of rank and title. "What care I for the skin! 'Tis the stuffing that matters," he would say. "And these jewelled popinjays that claim authority over us simple folk, what are they stuffed with but wind, feathers, and self-importance." This sturdy independence at first shocked Dick, accustomed as he was to think of his class as having a Divine right to pre-eminence and overlordship. But before he had been a day with Tom he began to realize how vigorous must be the roots of that life of which he and his kind were the fine flower. Tom was a regular mountain-torrent for talk. He would chatter for hours, once he realized Dick's appetite for information, about the ways of the poor, particularly those who stood outside the law. He had the same pride in his professional skill as Martin in his gunnery.

It was more important for Dick that Tom was a prince of his profession, one of the Upright Men. Though he did not divulge the fact, it soon became sufficiently obvious to Dick's sharp wits. Many villages lay on their route. Some they would go out of their way to avoid, for the sight of such scallywags on horseback might well provoke the suspicion of the local constables. At other times ragged men would spring up out of thin air, it seemed, at a sign from Tom: some would lead the horses round to the far side of the village, while Tom and Dick would march brazenly into an inn and call for refreshment. Dick was at first nervous of showing himself openly, for he had thrown off his disguise as being of no further use: but Tom, sensing his fears, would jerk a thumb over his shoulder, and Dick would see three or four unkempt men lounging around the door. He smiled grimly to think how the safety of the real was thus being unconsciously guarded by those who cared not a straw for its laws.

On several occasions, once in a village and twice on lonely upland stretches of road, masked men darted out at them and retired as hastily, seeing their ragged bodyguard. Each detachment of rogues would escort Tom and Dick for a few miles, padding tirelessly by their side; then they would melt away, and another would spring up as though Tom carried, not a cudgel, but a magic wand. A few words of weird jargon would pass between them and Dick's friend; then nothing would be heard but the clatter of hooves and the pad of feet. Travelling thus, they slipped through the widespread net of Sir Giles' agents, and on the third evening after Dick's escape from Clifford

the walls of London lay before him. Tom Tuttlesham
embraced him heartily, saying:

"Good speed, my young gamecock. 'Twere better
for my health that I enter not the city; but thou dost not
go unattended; my men will have thee under watch till
thou enterest thy noble lord's house. Ay me, though, I
would we were not to part: I could make a pretty thief
of thee with time and trouble."

Dick laughed and thanked Tom with all his heart.
Then he rode forward, seeing the strong, clever face of
Walsingham in his mind's eye, glad to think that the first
part of his mission was almost completed. And even as
his thoughts turned to Sir Francis his hand strayed to his
neck, and he went chill with dismay, for no cord lay
about it. The ring was gone! Where could he have lost
it? He was sure it had been safe in his keeping that morning. And without it how could he hope, all stained and
ragged and rapscallion-looking as he was, to gain audience
with the Queen's secretary? He was sitting his horse aim-
lessly, almost weeping in despair and vexation of spirit,
when there came a drumming of hooves behind him and
Tom hove again into sight. Dick was amazed to see his
merry eyes downcast and something very like a blush on
his tanned cheeks. He dismounted and came hesitatingly
up to Dick.

"Friend, I took a keepsake from thee on parting: but
when I came to examine it more closely I found signs on
it that made me think it were better to return it to thee."

He pressed something into Dick's hand and rode off
faster than he had come. Dick opened his hand. Sir
Francis Walsingham's ring lay in it. He moved on, mar-
velling at this strange creature, who could protect his friend
from death and steal the ring from his neck—and give it
back when he discovered its importance. Dick began to

realize that he was yet but a child in his knowledge of men. So musing, he passed through the gates of London Town, scarce conscious of the unobtrusive bodyguard which attended him, and enquired of a citizen the whereabouts of Sir Francis Walsingham's house.

The sun was showering its final largesse for the day upon the cramped streets when Dick dismounted, gave his horse and a silver coin to the leader of his tattered retinue, and limped wearily up to Sir Francis' door. Two pikemen, in bright liveries that showed the badge of the tigers, barred his way. He drew out the ring, and at sight of the tiger crest upon it the men lowered their weapons. The ring was an open sesame, clearing every obstruction from his path, till he found himself in a small audience chamber, confronting again the grizzled head and steel-point eyes of the Queen's secretary. The eyes regarded him frostily for a moment, then grew warm and welcoming.

"Why, if it is not my young gallant of the Salisbury road! Well met, Dick—Sir Richard Willoughby, I should call thee. I heard tell of thy father's death. A great good gentleman, and one whom this sore-troubled realm of ours could ill spare. Where hast thou been hiding these two years? Shouldst have come to Court. But I dare hazard from thy complexion thou hast been following the seaways of thy noble sire."

Dick gave him a brief account of his fortunes, noticing a grim glint in Walsingham's eyes when the name of Sir Giles was mentioned.

"But, 'tis not of my humble fortunes I came hither to speak, my lord," he proceeded. "I have matter of greatest import to the State for which I sue thy hearing."

"So-ho. Matters of State? Well, we shall discuss them none the worse over the supper-table. I pray thee honour me with thy company."

And the secretary led Dick with a friendly hand upon his shoulder into another room, where a rich banquet was laid out. Dick fell upon the viands whole-heartedly—he had not broken fast since that morning—and between mouthfuls told all he had heard from his concealment in the secret passage. He had scarcely begun his narrative when Walsingham interrupted him, beckoning an attendant to whom he whispered certain directions. The attendant hastened from the room, and Dick continued. Walsingham's eyes shone with a metallic light, his thin lips curved in an almost gloating smile; he nodded his head frequently as Dick unfolded to him the names of the chief conspirators, the details of their machinations. But he made no comment, even when Dick had finished: only sat statue-still in his chair, his food untasted, the tigerish expression deepening on his face. Dick was somewhat piqued by his silence, having expected gratitude, jubilation, swift action. Sir Francis, with his uncanny power of reading unspoken thoughts, presently started up from his immobility and clapped Dick on the shoulder.

"Young sir, thou hast done well. We are beholden to thee. Thou shalt not find the Council ungrateful. . . . So," he continued, speaking half to himself, "'tis as I knew. Babington, Ballard; an armada. We have not been asleep in London while thou wert bearding the lion in his den. Lion, say I? Scorpion, rather. Aye, thou tellest me little I knew not already."

Then, seeing the chagrin on Dick's open face: "Mistake me not. I would not belittle thy services. Thou art come as the coping-stone for my toilsomely obtained evidence. 'Tis the Queen that ever standeth in the way of her own safety. But she must believe now: she cannot but give credence to thee. So, conspiracy, we have thee on the hip!"

As he spoke, an elderly gentleman, clad in sombre richness, with a white beard and a somewhat pompous bearing, was ushered into the room.

"My lord Cecil," said Walsingham, "our troubles are at an end. We have here a young gentleman who hath unravelled the tangle for us."

Dick bowed low over the white, jewelled hand, his heart beating quicker to feel himself in the presence of William Cecil, Lord Burghley, the first statesman of the realm. Walsingham made him tell his whole story over again to the great man, who, unlike Sir Francis, interrupted so frequently and with such measured long-windedness that Dick was reduced to a positive fever of impatience and at the end burst out impulsively:

"My noble lords, I prithee if I have done aught of service, recompense me by allowing me to ride back posthaste with a troop of men."

"Not so fast, young man, not so fast," said Burghley, frowning. "These matters must be dealt with in decent order, and——"

"But, my lord," interrupted Dick rashly, "my friend Martin is in deadliest danger, and every moment wasted may increase it. I have a plan——"

Walsingham's voice cut like cold steel through Dick's stammering eagerness.

"Bethink you, Sir Richard; I allow no private life to stand against the common weal. Thy heart is froward and must be schooled to patience." Then, more kindly: "We need thee to convince the Queen. Thinkest thou she will give ear to thee if thou breakest into the presence in thy tatterdemalion guise? Nay, thou must curb thy ardour till we have made thee fit for the Court. Then, I warrant, thou wilt be of a figure to take majesty by storm. A handsome face and a gallant bearing carry ever more

weight with the Queen than our grey-beard wisdom, is't
not so, my lord Cecil?"

So it came about that Dick found himself, at ten o'clock
on the morrow, entering Whitehall Palace in brilliant
courtier dress, Cecil and Walsingham, the Queen's right
and left hands, walking on either side. The Lord Cham-
berlain himself escorted them through the guard chamber. At the door of the presence chamber a gentleman
in velvet and gold chain met them and announced their
names.

Dick's eyes were dazzled by the magnificent scene that
opened up as he followed in upon the heels of Burghley
and Walsingham. Grouped about the sumptuous apart-
ment were nobles, courtiers, gentlemen-ushers, officers of
the guard, colourful as a rose-garden in June. Attended by
her maids of honour dressed all in white, lovelier than
stately lilies, on a dais at the far end of the room sat the
Queen. She had outlived her girlish beauty, and an un-
romantic eye would have seen through her outworks of
peacock clothing, her frizzy auburn wig, and her thick-
painted face to the strange, vain, simpering, moody, reso-
lute creature they hid. But Dick's heart brimmed with
romance, and his eyes were dazzled. He could see nothing
but the Virgin Queen, the legendary figure of his heart,
a paragon of beauty and majesty.

Burghley led him up to Elizabeth and presented him.
He knelt, his head bowed low over the long beringed
fingers, quite unconscious of the stir his handsome presence
made among the courtiers, some of whom already were
whispering jealously among each other against this youth
whose beauty might oust former favourites from the
Queen's affection. He felt the royal hand lift up his face,
and found himself gazing into a pair of dark eyes that
started from boredom to interest on seeing him—eyes in

which a man's shrewdness mingled with an almost pathetic greed for admiration and love.

"Christopher," she said, in a mild voice, turning to a gentleman who stood near by, her favourite courtier, the Vice-Chamberlain, Sir Christopher Hatton, "why have we not beheld this pretty youth at Court before? Sir Richard, thy father's name was not unknown to us. Thou must stay by our side. We would have thee an officer of our guard."

And to Dick's blushing embarrassment he felt the jewelled hand lay his head on her knee and stroke his hair. At this point Burghley advanced and whispered a few words in the Queen's ear. Her brow wrinkled fretfully: she tossed her head, and exclaimed in a gruff, loud voice contrasting queerly with her previous mild tones:

"'Sdeath, wilt thou never be done plaguing me with thy urgent business and thy long face, my lord Cecil?"

The courtiers murmured an obsequious assent to her words. Burghley was not popular among them, for some resented his influence with the Queen, and others looked down upon him as an upstart—his family having but lately risen to title. Elizabeth quelled this murmur with a flash of her eye, and, ripping out one or two most unmaidenly oaths, strode into the privy chamber, followed by Burghley, Walsingham, and Dick.

Here Dick, prompted by the skilful questioning of Sir Francis, recounted his whole story. When he was done, Burghley said:

"Your Majesty must comprehend now the danger which threatens. There remaineth no shadow of doubt that this conspiracy, of which we have warned you ere now, is no phantasy of our imagination. If Elizabeth fall, England falls. We beseech you to give us orders in council for the apprehension of the conspirators; and your kinswoman, the Queen of Scots——"

A spasm of indecision and horror crossed the Queen's face, and she interrupted Burghley's measured speech.

"Thou shalt have thy orders; though my old bones do protest I am weary of life, and my heart could almost welcome the assassin's dagger that would free it of the cankering cares of this realm. As to my kinswoman, I am not decided. We shall see, we shall see. I have too much blood on my conscience. Sir Richard Willoughby," she concluded, in her stateliest manner, "you have put a Sovereign in your debt. See to it that she hath opportunity to repay thee."

She sealed the orders which Burghley held out all ready for her, and retired with a languishing backward glance at Dick.

CHAPTER XXIII

LEAVING Burghley at Court, Walsingham and Dick returned to the former's house. Dick was on tenterhooks to be off, and his noble friend made no delay to speed him on his journey. As they were rowed away from Whitehall Sir Francis informed Dick of the preparations which had already been made to capture the conspirators. Soldiers had been sent the night before to form a cordon, hidden in the woods, round Clifford Castle. Whether Sir Giles or any others of his associates were still there was matter for doubt. But it seemed probable that he must have returned to the castle to destroy the evidences of his complicity, and that he would not expect Sir Francis to strike so quickly. If he had left Hampshire he would find it difficult to pierce that wide-flung net of Walsingham's agents, who had orders to keep watch for a hook-nosed man, hunch-backed, with a lisp in his voice.

"As thou sayest, Dick," Walsingham remarked, " thy friend, if alive, is in great peril, and any offensive move on our part might well cause his death. I approve freely of the plan thou didst outline to me last night. The gear thou askedst for is already prepared at my house. Would I were journeying with thee! I would give one of my estates to behold the traitor's face when he sees——"

At this point they reached the house, where a troop of horse was awaiting. Dick leapt on to a lovely thoroughbred, very different from the sorry nag which had brought him to town, slung over his back a leather bag which Sir Francis fetched out of the house, waved his hand; then the whole cavalcade galloped headlong away on to the West road. As they tore along, the dust billowing behind them, Dick was free—almost for the first time since they had parted—to think of Martin at length: and his thoughts brought a cold sweat to his brow and whipped his heart raw. The ride was a dream of hurricane motion. It was as though an avenging wind swept down upon Clifford Castle. Twice they dismounted and swung up on to fresh horses, and such good speed did they make that they were in the New Forest as daylight failed, and challenged softly by the hidden sentries before nine o'clock.

Their officer informed Dick that, as far as he could tell, no one had got away from the castle and no suspicion of their own presence was felt there. Two of Sir Giles' men had been caught in the woods, trying to get back inside the walls, and they had let out the fact, after some rough persuasion, that their master was still in the castle and that Martin was alive, a prisoner there. Dick now took command. Word was whispered from man to man, and under cover of darkness the cordon tightened, advancing to within a hundred yards of the unconscious foe. Dick himself, with the officer and four men, crept inch by inch till they were under the deeper shadow of the walls. Then Dick hooted thrice like an owl, the signal he had agreed on with Cynthia, below the postern.

But the postern did not open, not even when he repeated the signal after an interval of breathless expectancy. A legion of fears knocked at his heart. Some harm must have befallen Cynthia: she could never fail him otherwise. He gave the signal yet a third time. No answering sound or movement. The postern and the walls stood moated about with a tomb-like silence. A scouting trooper brought word that he had heard mutters of voices from the ruined cottage. That entrance, then, was blocked to them. But Dick had foreseen the possibility that Cynthia's plan might miscarry and had made an alternative one. This he now proceeded to bring into use.

He and the officer muffled themselves more closely in their riding cloaks, shadowing their faces with the dark material. The four soldiers slipped out of sight between the walls and the moat. Then the two cloaked figures stepped boldly up to the postern and Dick knocked—two short raps, a pause, three more. Days after, recalling this action in cold blood, Dick was amazed at its audacity. So many things might have gone wrong. The conspirators' signal might well have been altered since Dick had heard it across the breathless gulf of evening: there might have been a password: the courtyard might have teemed with armed men; the conspirators all within the castle, or known to be all far away by now. But at the time, though he knew it to be a desperate expedient, he felt supremely clear-headed and self-confident: his mind had room for no other thoughts but the thought that Martin's life hung on the single fine thread of his own nerve.

Like other desperate expedients, it was carried through by the momentum of its audacity. Dick had scarcely finished rapping on the door when it yawned silently open. The two slipped through and in a trice flung themselves upon the man who had opened it. A pair of irresistible hands snuffed out the cry of alarm in his throat; a dagger rose and fell: there was a little gasping cough; and the first defences had fallen. The officer dragged the body by the heels out through the postern, where one of the soldiers at once fell to the grisly work of stripping it and donning its clothing himself. Dick had hardly edged round the courtyard and darted through a side door before this soldier was standing at the dead man's post, ready to avert the suspicions of any of the garrison who might come into the yard: while the remaining troopers were clustered without the postern to reinforce their comrade should his identity be discovered.

So far the luck had run all their way, thought Dick, as he skulked along through the devious dark passages towards Cynthia's room. But his heart misgave him. Had it not all been too easy? Was he walking through the blindfold darkness into just such another trap as had been laid for Martin and himself? The notion paralyzed him, so that he stood a moment in dazed panic, incapable of movement, like a climber who has lost his nerve on a narrow ledge and cannot take the next step up or down. Then he gripped his coward body, as it were by the scruff, and urged it forward. He was outside Cynthia's door. He scratched on it lightly—the old signal of their childhood days. He heard a tremulous little cry from within: footsteps faltered across the floor: the door opened. He was inside, in the safe haven that he must have to prepare for the final stage of his plan.

Cynthia's face, as he turned to her, shook the very centre of his heart. Her eyes were red with crying; there was an angry weal on her cheek-bone; and when he took her in his arms he felt warm blood through the tattered clothing on her back. But it was the expression in her eyes that stunned him most with fear. For they stared at him, dilated in panic, and her hands went trembling up before her, as though to ward him off. She could not have looked more terrified if he had been a ghost, he thought.

"Cynthia, my dear one, what it is? 'Tis I, Dick. I am come back to thee. Look not at me so, Cynthia."

Her body remained rigid and inhuman against his for a moment, then relaxed, and was racked with a storm of weeping. When the spasm was over she touched him and clung to him in wild relief, her voice still broken with sobs.

"Oh, Dick, is it really thou? They told me thou wert dead—and when thou camest in I thought, I thought thou wert——" She wept afresh.

"Nay, Cynthia, I am no ghost. Canst thou not feel me flesh and blood?"

"Surely some miracle hath brought thee back to me. But yestreen two men rode up—one had his arm bandaged—and told my uncle thou hadst been killed: they said something of a quarry; and he told me, with triumph in his voice: he hath cast all pretence to the winds."

In a flash Dick realized his luck, understood why the castle was left almost unguarded. The two ruffians who had set on him, fearing Sir Giles' murderous wrath if they admitted the failure of their mission, had pretended its success. Sir Giles verily believed him dead. Cynthia broke in on his thoughts.

"Dick, why do we delay? Hast thou brought help? They have taken Martin down into the dungeons, and I know not what they purpose to do with him."

"When did they take him?"

"Not an hour ago. I did my best, Dick. I besought mine uncle to have mercy, but he laughed in my face. He is like a madman. Then I flew at him with my little hunting knife, but he wrested it from me, and—and he whipped me."

Dick's eyes blazed with such a volcanic fire of rage that even Sir Giles might have felt fear if he could have seen him then.

"He whipped thee; ha? I have a tall score to reckon up with him: but this; perdie, he shall pay for it with a thousand pains."

"Oh, my dear, what canst thou do? He hath six men with him. I prithee endanger thyself no more for me.

Yet there is Martin. Perchance thou mightest surprise mine uncle, since he would believe thee a ghost, but——"

"Aye, we shall ghost him," muttered Dick grimly, "but not as thou thinkest."

And he rummaged in the leather bag he still carried with him, and took out two things—a shroud, such as corpses are buried in, stained hideously with mould, and a mask. Even Cynthia could not repress a cry of dismay when she saw him in these strange accoutrements: for the mask had been painted with phosphorus by an alchemist, an acquaintance of Walsingham, and cunningly fashioned so that it resembled a face all eaten away by disease—the face of the Shining Leper.

"Thou wilt find soldiers at the postern," whispered Dick urgently. "Lead them into the house; let them block up the holes when these rats begin to run. But let them not act till I give the sign—they know what it is; I must fright them out of the dungeon first. And tell the captain not to lay hand on Sir Giles: he is my prey."

Dick clutched the shroud about him, felt the dagger hidden under his arm, and stalked out of the room, practising a spectral gait. He had taken off his riding-boots, so that he moved noiselessly as death along the passage towards the stone stairs that led down to the dungeons. Underneath the livid mask his face was white-hot with rage: he could almost feel his fingers sinking into Sir Giles' neck. Suddenly he stopped dead, his hair rose on end, and his flesh crawled. For there, ten yards in front of him as he turned a corner, stood the Shining Leper, shrouded as though this moment risen from the grave, his face a blank, baleful wall of flesh. Dick started back, and as he did so the spectre seemed to cower away too: a tiny spring of relief began to bubble in Dick's heart: very slowly, for his reason depended on it, he raised his hands before his face. The spectre's face was blotted out. Dick advanced, but firmly now; and the fearful counterpart advanced to meet him. It was his own reflection in a mirror at the end of the passage.

Dick's revulsion was so great that he swayed against the wall, his knees all loosened. But a stifled groan from the hollow regions below strung him again to action. He went down the stair and silently opened the iron-studded door of the dungeon. A bloodshot light from torches and a brazier flickered like the fires of hell over dark figures grouped intent round a man strapped in an iron chair. It was Martin. His face dropped beads of sweat and his mouth was distorted: but the red beard still jutted out like a flag in defiance of his tormentors. Iron rods were glowing on the brazier, and some twisted devilry of iron was being applied to Martin even as Dick entered. Sir Giles was leaning negligently against the wall; but his face was maniac—all his venom and cruelty seemed to be boiling over in his eyes.

"What didst thou hear? Thy pretty young friend is dead—dead, dost thou understand? Thou wert better advised to open that stubborn mouth. This last chance thou hast before we use the burning irons to prise it open. What didst thou hear? Doth any other soul know what thou knowest? Speak, thou surly dog!" ·

Fearful was this subterranean scene that Dick took in at a glance. But more fearful far was the spectacle which battered on the eyes of the torturers as they spun round at a movement from Dick. A figure, unnaturally tall in the glowering half-light, clad in the vestments of decay, its face a dead end, a whited sepulchre of flesh surpassing all horror. For a second they stood stonily, as though Gorgon-struck: then broke before Dick's noiseless advance, shrieking, "The Leper! The Shining Leper!" and

THE TORTURE.

crushed through the door. As they went Dick lifted his voice in a bubbling, bloodcurdling wail that sent them stampeding wildly away into the grip of the soldiers posted about the castle, whose signal for action was this selfsame wail rising out of the ground at their feet.

Martin, half dead with pain and terror, struggled faintly at his bonds as the spectre approached. But it did not make to touch him; only, out of the ravaged desert of its face, came the tiniest whisper: " Be of good cheer : 'tis I, Dick." The mariner's eyes started almost out of his head. Dick's voice proceeding from that ghoulish face: his sufferings must have turned his wits, he thought, watching the figure stalking Sir Giles through the dungeon door. When the soldiers hurried down the stone stair they found the dungeon empty but for a red-bearded mariner slumped in a dead swoon over the arm of an iron chair.

While they were knocking off his manacles a strange chase was in progress through the dim corridors. Sir Giles retreated, step by step, eyes fixed upon his pursuer. Dick advanced, never hastening the deliberation of his stride, even when Sir Giles' nerve seemed to break and he fled frantically a dozen paces, only to resume his nightmare-slow retreat as though held by a cord of fascination to the follower. Walsingham had told Dick that Sir Giles must be taken alive. But it was not Walsingham's authoritative voice and eyes that were in command now; it was two dark eyes red with weeping, a broken voice, a body hurt by the savage whip. Not the Queen and her whole Privy Council could have restrained Dick then from his revenge.

So the slow-motion hunt proceeded, till Sir Giles, apparently cornered in an upper room, whipped out a key, flung open a panel, and stumbled up the stairway of the tower. He must have been crazed with fear indeed, for he did not even seek to lock this door behind him. Dick, following leisurely up to the tower-top, his prey secured at last, realized too late that craftiness, not panic, had made his pursuit so easy. Emerging into the cool night air, he saw Sir Giles standing on the battlement, a few feet away, his face swept of its mimic terror, swept of everything but a pure fire of hate.

"So, my pretty cousin, thou'rt cozened indeed," he snarled, and laughed a madman's laugh. "Didst think thou couldst fool me with thy childish gewgaws, thy shrouds and shining paint? Shouldst not whisper the truth when thou playest bogey: thy surly friend's eyes betrayed thee. And now have I led thee where I may settle my reckoning without interference. Thou hast crossed me at every turn. Thou shalt go with me the rest of my journey."

He sprang off the battlement at Dick's throat, and a furious encounter began under the cloud-racked sky. Dick was so stupefied by his enemy's change of face that he was caught unawares, encumbered in the shroud; and his dagger was whisked away ere he had poised it for a blow. Sir Giles' strength was unnatural to his shrivelled, hunchback frame. He seized Dick and propelled him, wildly struggling, towards the platform's edge. Dick was but an inch or so from that precipice when his heels caught on the stonework, and shoving madly at it he hurled himself back into safety, crashing with his foe on to the leaden floor. There they scrimmaged like two tigers, twisting, clawing, biting, in the blind ecstasy of hate. Dick's muscles, trained by the rigours of the galley, the triumphant strength which sea service had given him, slowly came into the ascendant. Sensing this, Sir Giles called upon the supernatural reserves of his maniac fury; flung

Dick off him; staggered to his feet; fastened upon his reeling foe; and bore him once more backward towards the lip of disaster. Dick fought every inch, and with a convulsive twist wrenched the other's body between him and the battlement. But he felt his strength dying in him; and he had resigned himself to his doom when his right hand, momentarily released to seek a firmer hold, closed upon the haft of a dagger, offered to him apparently by the intangible darkness. He drove it upward. Blood gushed over him. He thrust his foe into the abyss. Sir Giles' hands clawed at him: but other hands, gripping him from behind, saved him from being plucked over the edge. Cynthia had followed the deadly procession up to the tower, and, finding Dick's dagger on the floor, intervened at the last split second of time. A sullen splash from the viewless depths below told them the end of an inveterate enemy, the end of their troubles, the beginning of happiness.

EPILOGUE

Now we must say good-bye to Dick, to Cynthia, and to Martin. They had played a part in history, and they were glad to retire into the shelter of their own peace. Only once more did Dick and Martin step out on to a wider stage. The other conspirators were taken. Sir Francis saw to that. Nor was Dick's interview with him as stormy as he feared: Walsingham rated him roundly for having taken Sir Giles' punishment into his own hands, but the twinkle in his eyes belied the severity of his tone. And the Queen's gratitude was almost embarrassing to Dick, who only wanted the enjoyment of his own estate. The conspiracy was scotched; and we know from the history books what happened to the lovely, luckless Queen of Scots. But one danger still remained. The threat of the Armada hung like a storm-cloud in the offing. It found our heroes, with every true man in the country, Protestant or Catholic, ready to face it when it burst.

Dick was undisputed master of his inheritance at last. And he taxed its resources to the utmost, equipping two armed ships to swell the Queen's forces. When the pinnace came fluttering into the Channel and beacons sowed the sparks of war over all England, Dick and Martin went on board and fought their last fight with the Spaniard. They lived scatheless through that long week of manœuvre and cannonade. The Dons in Calais Roads beheld a red-bearded giant and a wiry, golden-haired youth among the men that launched the fire-ships to harry them out of their security. And when the galleons blundered away north amidst the rising waves, to find cold comfort on the crags of Scotland and Ireland, Dick and Martin were there to speed them on their way.

So Dick came back to Willoughby Hall and to Cynthia, where his treasure was. They were wedded about the time when the remains of Philip's proud fleet limped back to him. And neither the splendour of the Court nor the lure of western Eldorados could ever wean Dick from her side again. Martin, too, determined that his seafaring days were over. He settled down at Willoughby Hall, and, taking Sally to wife, presently peopled it with a brood of lusty carrot-haired children who plagued and teased him to his heart's content. Many a discharged sailor, tramping the roads sick at heart with the ingratitude of rulers who cast his like aside when their usefulness was done, received comfort and fresh hope at the hands of the generous young master of Willoughby Hall and his beautiful consort. Many a desperate encounter was fought over again in its lighted hall when Dick and Martin and some wandering mariner foregathered over brimming tankards. Sometimes a tall, twinkling rogue would stride into the courtyard, and Dick would come running out, crying, " Tom Tuttlesham, not in prison yet?" and would chaff him unmercifully about a certain ring which had altered the destinies of England.

There we may leave them to their lasting joy; to the satisfaction of those who have ridden out the stormy weather with courage and made their landfall—

" the fond,
The faithful, and the true."